"Tell M[...]
Heart [...]

Carlo urged.

Serena laughed, a soft husky sound that almost destroyed his control. "Tell me where *you* think it was."

"I dared to hope it was close to mine. But now—" He hesitated, feeling the thin ice beneath him.

She frowned. "But now?"

"How can I feel close to you when you still act as my enemy? Now that we've found each other, surely you see that the moment has come for you to tell me where to find my daughter, to give her back to me." He was praying frantically for her understanding.

But almost at once he realized that it had all gone wrong. He felt her stiffen in his arms, and a mask of caution and reserve obliterated the light that glowed on her face. She looked at him silently for a moment, before trying to push him away. "I see," she said quietly.

Dear Reader:

Welcome to Silhouette Desire – provocative, compelling, contemporary love stories written by and for today's woman. These are stories to treasure.

Each and every Silhouette Desire is a wonderful romance in which the emotional and the sensual go hand in hand. When you open a Desire, you enter a whole new world – a world that has, naturally, a perfect hero just waiting to whisk you away! A Silhouette Desire can be light-hearted or serious, but it will always be satisfying.

We hope you enjoy this Silhouette today – and will go on to enjoy many more.

Please write to us:

Jane Nicholls
Silhouette Books
PO Box 236
Thornton Road
Croydon
Surrey
CR9 3RU

LUCY GORDON
ON HIS HONOR

Silhouette Desire

Originally Published by Silhouette Books
a division of
Harlequin Enterprises Ltd.

First published in Great Britain in 1992
by Silhouette Books, Eton House, 18-24 Paradise Road,
Richmond, Surrey TW9 1SR

© Lucy Gordon 1991

Silhouette, Silhouette Desire and Colophon are
Trade Marks of Harlequin Enterprises B.V.

ISBN 0 373 58375 3

22-9203

Made and printed in Great Britain

LUCY GORDON

met her husband-to-be in Venice, fell in love the first evening and got engaged two days later. After seventeen years they're still happily married and now live in England with their three dogs. For twelve years Lucy was a writer for an English women's magazine. She interviewed many of the world's most interesting men, including Warren Beatty, Richard Chamberlain, Roger Moore, Sir Alec Guinness and Sir John Gielgud.

Other Silhouette Books by Lucy Gordon

Silhouette Desire

Take All Myself
The Judgement of Paris
A Coldhearted Man
My Only Love, My Only Hate
A Fragile Beauty
Just Good Friends
Eagle's Prey
For Love Alone
Vengeance Is Mine
Convicted of Love
The Sicilian

Silhouette Special Edition

Legacy of Fire
Enchantment in Venice
Bought Woman

A Special Letter From Lucy Gordon

Dear Reader:

There was never any doubt that my *Man of the World* would be Italian. My love affair with Italy began in my teens, with an addiction to the opera. It was years before I managed to scrape together enough money to visit the country of my dreams, and it was as wonderful as I'd known it would be. There, just as I'd always imagined them, were the sun, the wine, the music, the laughter and the atmosphere of brooding sensuality. Above all, there were the marvelous Italian men—one of whom became my husband.

I discovered that there's actually no such thing as an Italian man. There are Venetians, Romans, Florentines, Neopolitans, Sicilians, and many more, and they're as varied as if they belonged to different nations. I've explored these differences in several Silhouette books. The hero of my last Desire, *The Sicilian,* had an elemental quality that he drew from his wild surroundings. By contrast, Carlo, the hero of *On His Honor* is very much a Roman. He's descended from a race that once ruled the earth, and he has all the arrogance and pride of the ancient Caesars. His stern sense of honor makes him incapable of a mean action, but it can also make him rather rigid. He has to almost lose his life before he can find his love. That's the "Italian" man— prepared to risk everything to gain his treasure. And nothing is more romantic than that.

Sincerely,

Lucy Gordon

One

He was dreaming, and in his dream he saw a face that had haunted him for years, the face of a young woman with light brown hair and large, serious eyes. He'd seen it vivid with youthful eagerness, and fierce with scorching contempt. And once, in a never-to-be-forgotten moment, he'd thought he'd seen it alight with a passionate, unspoken feeling that had matched his own.

"Serena..." Carlo said her name aloud, and on the word the waking dream vanished and he found himself seated at his desk amid the austere luxury of his office in the heart of Rome. He was still holding the cable that had arrived a few minutes earlier. It declared, with bleak formality, that his wife, Dawn, had died suddenly in England.

The untimely end of a beautiful, vivacious woman had filled Carlo with shock and pity, followed by sadness at the memory of his one-time infatuation for her, and how it had ended. She'd answered his boyish passion with greed, deviousness and infidelity. At last his love had worn out, leaving only numbness and a determination to cling to the dreadful, hollow marriage for the sake of their daughter.

Now Dawn was gone, and her cousin Serena had cabled the news rather than call and speak to him. She couldn't have said more clearly that she still hated and despised him.

He called England. The phone was answered by a woman he didn't know. "This is Carlo Valetti," he said. "I want to speak to Serena Fletcher."

He heard the woman repeat his message faintly, as if she'd turned away. There was a long silence, but at last he heard, "This is Serena."

Her voice sounded deeper on the telephone, but otherwise it was just as he remembered, confident but with an undertone of huskiness that affected him. "I've just received your cable," he said. "Please tell me what happened."

"Dawn contracted pneumonia. She seemed to be recovering—but then she had a heart attack."

"How long was she ill?"

"Four days."

"Four days—and you didn't call me?" he grated.

"Dawn begged me not to. She didn't want you."

He controlled his anger. "And my daughter? How is she?"

"Distressed, as you'd expect, but I'm comforting her."

"Let me speak to her."

"I'm afraid you can't."

"What do you mean, *I can't?*"

"She's asleep and I want her to stay that way."

Years of having his slightest wish instantly obeyed had left him unprepared to deal with frustration. "Fetch my daughter to the phone at once," he commanded in a voice that would have sent his employees scuttling for cover.

Her voice reached him, equally firm. "Louisa cried herself to sleep all last night and she's worn out. Please understand, once and for all, that I am not waking her."

The thought of his little Louisa crying her heart out hurt him so much that for a moment he was unable to speak. He tightened his hand on the receiver, fighting for composure. Dawn had been a poor mother, smothering her daughter with sentimental effusions when it suited her, and neglecting her when something more interesting turned up. But she was the only mother Louisa had ever known, and now she was gone. It should have been himself who cradled the child in his arms, soothing her sobs. For a moment he hated Serena.

But his voice, when he spoke again, gave no inkling of this. He'd recovered his balance enough to try tact. "Serena, I know you think you're doing the right thing, but surely you understand that I'm the person she needs? Who can comfort her better than her father?"

The silence from the other end lasted so long he thought she'd hung up. "Serena?"

"I'm here. I'm sorry, I can't see things as you do. Dawn left her daughter in my care and made me promise to keep her."

"Perhaps her father has something to say about that," he said through gritted teeth.

"Dawn made a will, leaving me as Louisa's sole guardian. I'm keeping her, Carlo. I gave my word."

"Just what did Dawn tell you?" he asked slowly.

"You must know what she told me. You were going to throw her out of her home, divorce her and never let her see Louisa again."

"Serena—"

"I can't imagine what kind of a monster a man would have to be to make a threat like that. I only know I'm glad she escaped in time. She begged me to keep Louisa safe, and that's what I'm going to do. Don't come after her, Carlo. You won't find her." Serena choked off abruptly, and Carlo wondered about the tremor he'd heard in her voice.

"It's useless talking about this now," he said harshly. "We'll speak some more when I reach England."

"You're coming here?" She sounded dismayed.

"Certainly," he snapped, adding chill irony, "even a monster like myself has enough sense of propriety to attend his wife's funeral." He heard her draw in her breath. "Kindly tell me when it is to be," he said.

"Next Tuesday," Serena said, and told him the time and the place.

"Thank you. I'll check that."

"Meaning that you think I'd lie about it?" she demanded furiously.

"You've just drawn up the battle lines. Don't blame me if I treat you as an enemy."

He put down the phone abruptly. His handsome face was hard with anger, but that was the only outward sign of his inner turmoil. He'd learned control because it was vital for a man who had to guide a racing car at high speed, run a huge company and endure existence with a faithless wife. But Serena could threaten that control. At a distance of five years and a thousand miles, the thought of her still disturbed him. Their conversation had crackled with tension and hostility, but beneath it some other, unacknowledged feeling had vibrated.

He rose and went to the window, staring down at the busy traffic of the Via Veneto. Dawn had loved this fashionable street with its profusion of expensive shops and restaurants. In fact she had loved every part of the glamorous life-style that her husband's money had been able to buy her.

The money came from Valetti Motors, the creation of the legendary Italian racing driver, Emilio Valetti, who'd won the World Championship six times and then founded a firm that would keep his name alive. He manufactured elegant, state-of-the-art sports cars to sell at top prices to the very wealthy. But he also created racing cars, which he entered for the World Championship, with frequent success.

Carlo had grown up in a home dominated by his father's fame. He'd become a racing driver himself and for a few years had enjoyed the colorful life. He'd been a handsome boy, tall, slim and strong, with dark hair and eyes and enough youthful high spirits to pass for lightheartedness. In truth he had never been genuinely light of heart, and the years of pain and struggle since then had brought out a saturnine quality in his looks. He was thirty-three, but worry had etched lines of bitterness about his eyes and given his sensual mouth a twist of cynicism.

He'd been twenty-two when he met Dawn Fletcher, and she a few years older. He'd gone to Monza for the Italian Grand Prix, and there she'd been, with another driver. She'd strolled into the pit while Carlo's car was being prepared, and immediately apologized for coming to the wrong pit. Carlo had been dazzled by her beauty, her vivacity and her air of sophistication. In less than a month they were married.

He'd been a callow boy, too immature to look behind the surface glitter to the calculating woman underneath. Her "mistake" had been no accident. She'd deliberately come looking for the heir to the Valetti fortune. Carlo knew that, because years later, during one of their cold, bitter rows, she had told him so. Sometimes Dawn's spite had overcome her self-interest.

His father had died soon afterward, and he'd left racing to take over the running of the firm. What he discovered horrified him. Behind its glittering facade, Valetti Motors was a mess. The commercial side existed only to finance the racing, and for years Emilio had recklessly squandered money on his pet projects, turning a blind eye to the dangerous imbalance in the books. Carlo began a tough campaign of cutting out waste. Those who'd lived well at the firm's expense squealed with outrage, and his reputation for ruthlessness was born. He didn't care. It was useful in convincing the banks that he could be trusted with the huge loans necessary to bring the firm around.

He did some fast growing up, and in the process he lost what little he'd ever had of his wife. She'd married a boy and she found herself with a tense, serious-minded man. She didn't love him enough to identify herself with his struggle, and she rapidly became bored. When he asked her to curb her extravagant life-style, she grew enraged.

Only Louisa gave purpose to his life. He'd adored the little mite from the moment of her birth, and in the next three years that love had grown and deepened.

One day, after a particularly fierce row about Dawn's enormous gambling debts, Carlo had come home to find them both missing, and a note from Dawn to say she'd gone to visit her family in England. He knew she and a young cousin had been raised by grandparents, but Dawn hadn't seemed close to her family. She'd never been back to see them, or invited them to Italy, and this sudden flight, without a word of warning, struck him as ominous. Dawn was letting him know that she could and would deprive him of his daughter if he made a fuss about money. He'd hurried to England and pursued her to Delmer, the sleepy midland village where her relatives lived.

It was buried in the heart of the country, surrounded by gentle hills. In different circumstances Carlo might have been struck by the atmosphere of peace and beauty. As it was, he was driven to distraction by the fact that the nearest train stopped twenty miles away, forcing him to hire a car and get lost in the winding lanes.

He'd finally arrived late in the afternoon, exasperated and irritable, to find Dawn stretched out in a hammock in the garden of a large, old house. She'd looked up and smiled, not at him, but at her own cleverness in luring him after her. "Darling, I thought you'd never get here," she purred.

"Where's Louisa?" he demanded at once.

Dawn shrugged her elegant, Armani-clad shoulders. "I expect Serena's taken her off somewhere."

"You *expect?* You don't even know where your daughter is, and that doesn't worry you?"

"Why should it? If she's not with Serena, she'll be with the grandparents. They all adore her."

"Unlike her mother," he said grimly.

"That's not fair. I spent an exhausting day yesterday buying her clothes at the loveliest little children's boutique. And instead of being pleased, she got tearful and naggy and I had to bring her home early."

"She's three years old," he reminded her. "She hasn't yet learned to equate happiness with expensive clothes, and I hope she never does."

Dawn groaned. "Oh Lord, not another row about my bills."

"I didn't come here to argue, but to collect Louisa and go straight home," he declared flatly.

"That'll be very rude and hurtful to my grandparents, but I suppose you don't care about that," she said languidly.

His mouth tightened. He knew she cared little about her grandparents, but she was adept at shifting her ground in order to put him in the wrong.

"I don't mean to be rude—" he began to say, but stopped at the sight of Louisa scampering through the trees of a little wood that bordered the garden. Overwhelmed with joy, he opened his arms to her and she ran happily into them. For a moment he forgot everything except the pleasure of snuggling his face against her soft, sweet warmth and hearing her chuckle in his ear.

"For heaven's sake!" Dawn exclaimed, exasperated. She pulled the child away from him. "That lovely new dress. It cost a fortune, and look at it now." She began to brush bits of dried grass from the dress, glowering at the little girl, whose smile vanished as she sensed the atmosphere grow cold.

"Don't fuss over the child," Carlo told her. "What does it matter how she looks while she's playing?"

At that moment he saw a young woman emerging through the trees. She was little more than a girl, with soft brown hair that had been casually pinned up. She wore a faded cotton top that left her arms bare, and old jeans cut off just below the knee, revealing slim brown calves and bare feet. He wasn't a poetic man, but the thought flitted through his mind that she was like a wood sprite. "There you are," she called to Louisa, who scampered over to her. "Why did you run off, you monkey?"

"You see, I told you Serena had her safe," Dawn said.

"Apparently she didn't," Carlo retorted with quiet anger. He rose politely as Serena approached with Louisa.

"Serena darling, this is my wicked husband," Dawn said mischievously. "He managed to tear himself away from work for five minutes to come and find me."

Serena didn't laugh. She offered Carlo her hand, and he took it, feeling its softness against his palm, giving him an unexpected shock. With her free hand she brushed back a lock of hair that had fallen over her face. She greeted Carlo gravely, while her green eyes looked him up and down in an appraising manner that annoyed him. He was used to sizing people up, not the other way around. "Well?" he said coolly, "do you think I'm wicked?"

It was the kind of labored witticism that was foreign to his nature, and he couldn't imagine what had made him utter it. She completed his discomfort by releasing her hand and saying quietly, "I'm not sure."

The knowledge that he was behaving awkwardly made him say in a curt tone, "My wife assured me Louisa was safe in your care. I didn't expect to find her wandering on her own."

The sudden color in her cheeks was like wild roses. "I'm sorry," she said in a slightly husky voice. "I stopped to admire a plant, and when I looked up again she'd wandered off."

"Children of that age normally do. That's why they need watching." He could have kicked himself for the surly words.

"I said I was sorry," she protested. "This is a private wood, and it's fenced. She couldn't have got out." She picked Louisa up. "Come on, let's see if we can find some ice cream."

She walked away without another word, leaving him cursing his own clumsiness. Dawn had watched the little scene in high glee. "You really are a charmer, aren't you?" she jeered.

Her grandparents, Liz and Frank, came out of the house, and he was enveloped in greetings and introductions. He liked the old people at once, and it was impossible to depart with Louisa as quickly as he'd planned. "You must stay for Serena's wedding," Liz said eagerly, and he found himself agreeing.

At supper his eyes strayed to Serena, who seemed coolly unaware of him. She'd abandoned her shabby outfit of the afternoon in favor of a flowing Indian muslin dress with a dappled green pattern, reinforcing the impression of a wood creature. She had a slight facial resemblance to Dawn, but whereas her cousin relied on the beauty parlor and the couturier, Serena was entirely natural. Dawn's hair was skillfully tinted the same perfect blond all over, and firmly lacquered into place. Serena's was bleached by the sun so that the top layer was a shade lighter than the rest, and so silky that no pins could imprison it for long. Carlo watched in fascination as a stray lock persistently escaped, falling down beside her soft cheek. Then he realized what he was doing and reddened, looking around the table to see if anyone had noticed him. But they were chattering.

After supper he found her alone on the porch. It seemed a good moment to mend his fences and he seized it, saying something pleasant about her coming marriage.

"Andrew will be here in a couple of days," she said.

"I look forward to meeting him," he responded politely. "Does he live far away?"

"No, just in the village, but he's away buying stock. He owns a hardware shop."

Remembering the rundown little shop from his drive through the village, he spoke his mind abruptly. "You can't live on what that place makes, surely?"

"Andrew thinks there are more important things in life than commerce," she said firmly. "And so do I."

Now he knew what Dawn had told her about him. "I hope you'll both be very happy," he said formally, and went inside.

He told himself how disagreeable she was, but later, when he slipped upstairs to look in on Louisa, he heard soft voices coming from inside her room. Pausing in the doorway, he saw Serena sitting on the child's bed, hugging her and whispering as though they shared a secret. Louisa was snuggled happily in her arms, and he thought how right they looked together. He'd never seen Dawn hold her child like that.

To his surprise he found himself enjoying the visit. The Fletcher's house was a cosy family home, and the old people welcomed him with open arms. He was touched to notice how devoted Liz and Frank were to each other, demonstrating their affection in front of the family without embarrassment. Now in their seventies, they had a lifetime of love behind them, and they let it flow freely over everyone they met, filling their home with happiness.

On the day after his arrival they all went to a dance in the village hall. He concentrated on mastering the unfamiliar country dances, determined not to look awkward.

"Don't scowl at me. It isn't my fault," came a teasing voice.

He looked and saw Serena opposite him, her eyes full of laughter. "What do you mean?" he demanded.

"The way you're scowling."

"That's concentration. I've never done this before."

"No one will care if you make a few mistakes."

"I don't mean to make any," he insisted.

At that very moment he collided with the vicar's wife, a large, jolly lady. They clutched each other wildly while Serena doubled up with laughter, and he scowled at her in outraged dignity. But then suddenly he was laughing, too. As the dance ended, he disentangled himself, apologized to his fellow victim and let Serena lead him to the makeshift bar. They got long, cool drinks and wandered out into the fresh air.

She was still chuckling. "I'm going to tell Louisa about this," she warned. "The next time you get cross with her she can picture you clinging on to poor Mrs. Brady."

"I'm never cross with her," he said truthfully.

"Oh no, not you," she laughed. "I'll bet the poor little mite has to do everything just so."

He was about to dispute this when he noticed that one curling lock had come free and was dancing about her face. Without even thinking he took it and pinned it back. He knew a slight shock as his fingers brushed her soft cheek. She glanced up quickly, an almost startled look in her eyes, but it was gone at once.

The little band began to play a waltz. They danced it together and she was like spring sunshine in his arms. There was a confused pain somewhere around his heart. He didn't understand it, but when the dance was ended he excused himself abruptly and left her. He didn't dance with Serena again that night, and before he went to bed he resisted the temptation to listen outside Louisa's door to hear if Serena was whispering secrets with his child.

The Fletchers had put his things in Dawn's room, and he was too embarrassed to explain that at home they slept apart. As she came from the bathroom that night he saw that she was in a flimsy nightgown with a plunging neck. That and her musky perfume told him that she wanted to demonstrate that she could bring him back to her whenever she chose. But it was too blatant, and his pride revolted.

He turned away to look out of the window, and saw a slim, youthful figure drifting through the garden. Her hair swung free about her shoulders. As he watched she flung her head back and spread her arms wide as if greeting the moon. Her eyes were closed. She was in some private world entirely of her own, where no one else existed, and for a moment he had a strange desolate feeling, as if she had snubbed him.

When he looked back on that visit Carlo could remember only moments that stood out as if illuminated by lightning.

There was the moment Serena's fiancé arrived. Andrew was a kindly, inoffensive young man, but everything about him had irritated Carlo to the point of madness.

Andrew was innocently proud of the humdrum little shop with the flat above, where he would take his bride to live. He apparently saw nothing incongruous about limiting Serena's horizons to the latest metal alloy, but Carlo saw it, and the thought enraged him as much as the sight of a wild bird in a cage would have done.

He tried to discuss business and was disconcerted when Andrew hung admiringly on his every word. Carlo's occasional caustic comments seemed to pass him by. But they didn't pass Serena by. Once he overheard them talking. "I can't imagine why you don't like him, darling," Andrew protested. "It's very kind of him to advise me."

"He's not advising you," she said hotly. "He's making a fool—making fun of you."

"Nonsense. What difference can it make to him?"

What difference can it make to him? That question increasingly troubled Carlo, but he wouldn't look at the answer. He was too afraid.

One day he'd come into the lounge unexpectedly to find Serena standing there in a luxurious wedding dress, surrounded by her admiring friends. "There now, you see I was right," Dawn was saying. "It looks perfect."

Carlo guessed who'd chosen this sophisticated creation, and a burning resentment rose in him. The brilliant white satin and lace, and the glittering tiara looked wrong on Serena, who should have gone to her wedding in the colors of nature, with briar roses in her hair and a single flower in her hand.

"This is our wedding present," Dawn informed him. "It cost a fortune, but you won't mind about that, will you, darling?"

As so often before, she'd put him in an impossible position. He got out of it as best he could, saying quickly, "Clothes are your department. I don't inter-fere." He knew he sounded surly, and read the confirmation in Serena's face, which was rosy with embarrassment at having, apparently, imposed on him.

"I can't accept this," she said quickly. "Besides, the wedding's going to be a very simple affair."

"Nonsense, you've got to dress up properly," Dawn insisted. "Louisa and I will be done up to the nines."

"You?" The word burst from Carlo involuntarily.

"I'm going to be the matron of honor and Louisa's going to be a bridesmaid."

"She's too young," he said firmly, thinking of his daughter being asked to stand still for ages, probably getting bored.

But Louisa pulled on his hand. "I've got such a pretty dress, Papa," she confided blissfully.

He shrugged, feeling awkward and outnumbered. "Of course, if that's what you want." He turned away, wishing he could escape from England and the mysterious "something" that was threatening him like a dark cloud, growing larger and more fearful every day.

He felt a touch on his arm and looked down to see a young woman. She was sturdily built with a pleasant, unremarkable face, and bright red hair. "I'm Patricia," she told him. "I just wanted to say that I'll keep an eye on Louisa and whisk her out if she looks tired or bored."

"I'm very grateful," he said, meaning it. "But aren't you going to be a bridesmaid?"

"Oh, no." She gave a deprecating laugh. "I'd just be like a suet pudding next to Serena. Don't you think she looks wonderful in that dress?"

"No," he said with revulsion, "I don't."

"Well, I do," she retorted indignantly, "and what's more, Andrew will." The next moment a blush suffused Patricia's face right up to the roots of her hair, and she hurried away.

That night Dawn said, "I don't know what's the matter with you. You can't be civil to anybody."

"It worries me to be away from the firm for so long."

"Oh, the firm, the firm. Why don't you go back to the damned firm? Just make sure you leave me some money. In fact, leave me a lot. I want to take Louisa for a little holiday."'

"Where?" he demanded quickly.

She shrugged. "Anywhere. Look, it'll be the French Grand Prix in a few weeks' time. Suppose we meet you there?"

He regarded her cynically. "And suppose you didn't turn up?"

She shrugged. "Would that be such a tragedy? Let's take a rest from each other. It'll do wonders for our marriage."

"It wouldn't do wonders for Louisa to be dragged from pillar to post all over Europe," he said bitingly. "I prefer to keep the two of you with me."

He gazed out into the garden. Serena always walked there last thing at night, and after a moment she appeared, strolling gracefully in the moonlight, looking more than ever a creature of the wild. Carlo held his breath knowing he should avert his eyes but unable to do so.

And then Andrew appeared between the trees, and the next moment Serena was running across the grass to him. Carlo drew in his breath, thinking how awkwardly Andrew embraced her, as though he had no idea of the value of what he held. No man had the right to kiss such a woman in that tentative way. He should crush her against him and overwhelm her with his passion until she gasped and he felt her slim body tremble against his in eager response.

Carlo became aware that he was holding the windowsill tightly enough to hurt, and sweat stood out on his brow. He wanted to groan aloud at the catastrophe that had come upon him. But it was too late. It had always been too late.

Next morning he called his office. After a terse conversation he faced the family and declared that a crisis at work would force him to return to Rome immediately, taking Dawn and Louisa with him. "But she's going to be a bridesmaid," Liz protested.

That had been the hardest part, depriving his darling of her treat. But he was running scared. He didn't dare to stay another moment in Serena's company, but he couldn't risk leaving Louisa behind in case he never saw her again. He dug his heels in and the family erupted around him.

The confrontation with Serena was the worst memory, written in fire. She caught him alone, shutting the door so that they could have privacy. "At least let Louisa stay," she protested. "It can't make any difference to you."

"That's for me to say," he replied, tight-lipped. "I'm leaving and I'm taking my wife and child with me."

"And suppose Dawn doesn't want to go?"

"She'll go."

She drew in her breath. "That has to be the most tyrannical, overbearing..."

"You know nothing about it," he shouted. He forced himself to calm down and added, "I've told you, there's a crisis in my firm, and I'm needed. My family goes where I do."

"Crisis my foot!" she exploded furiously. "There's no crisis. If there was, your firm would have called you instead of waiting for you to call them."

He knew it. He should have gone into the village to call his assistant and arrange to be called back, but he'd been too desperate to be subtle. He fell back on chilly formality. "It would be better if you didn't speak of matters you know nothing about," he announced.

"How convenient," she jeered. "How nice to be able to arrange life just as you want."

He stared at her, thinking wildly, *If I could do that, I'd never have met you, I wouldn't be here now to be tempted by your soft tousled hair that looks as if you've just risen from a night of love, your green eyes full of mystery and your voice with its husky note that drives me mad.*

"If you'll excuse me, I have to get ready," he snapped.

But she got between him and the door, leaning with her back to it so that he couldn't pass without touching her. "I won't excuse you," she blazed. "You walk all over people, and you don't even have the guts to tell the truth about why you're going."

He paled, thinking she'd divined his secret, but she rushed on, "Why didn't you say at the start that we're beneath your notice?"

"That's nonsense."

"Oh, no, it isn't! Who wants to hang around for a village wedding when they could be making money?"

Goaded beyond endurance, he seized her shoulders and pulled her away from the door, holding her tightly. "Listen to me," he said intently. "If you had any sense there wouldn't be a wedding. You're not the wife for Andrew."

"What do you know about it?" she demanded breathlessly.

"I know this. Your friend Patricia is in love with him, and she'd make him far happier than you will." Unaware that a new note had come into his voice, he said emphatically, "Don't do it, Serena. For your own sake and his, *don't marry him.*"

She opened her mouth to answer, but no sound came. She was staring at him in silent amazement. He tried not to look at her parted lips, tried not to think of them. But he couldn't stop his eyes meeting hers, and the shattered dawning of comprehension he saw in them was almost his undoing. His heart began to pound in his chest, so loudly that he was sure she must hear it. He forced himself to release her. The marks of his fingers showed plainly against her bare arm.

He discovered that he was breathing hard. "I'm going now," he said slowly. "I have preparations to make."

But before he could move, the door was flung open and Louisa rushed in and flung herself against him. "Papa, Papa, please let me stay," she begged.

"I'm afraid you can't, darling. We have to go, all of us."

Her lower lip trembled. "But I want to be a bridesmaid."

"You can be a bridesmaid another time," he said desperately.

"I want to be one now." Louisa had begun to cry. "*Please,* Papa."

"Let her stay for pity's sake," Serena urged.

With his nerves in shreds he snapped at her, "Keep out of it!" He picked up Louisa. It was the first time he'd denied her anything, and her tears tore him apart. For a moment he almost gave in, but just in time he looked up and saw Dawn over the child's shoulder, and the malicious look on her face strengthened his resolve. "Don't cry, *piccina,*" he whispered. "When we get home I'll buy you that big Columbine doll."

"I don't want a doll," she wept. "I want to be a bridesmaid."

A shudder went through Carlo as he held her tenderly against him, and he hid his face against her hair to conceal the fact that his own eyes were pricking. Beneath the chill restraint of his normal manner, he was a Latin with a Latin's emotional nature, and it was destroying him now. He knew if he didn't end this scene soon he would yield, and regret it for the rest of his life. "Well you can't," he said, speaking roughly to hide the huskiness in his voice.

"Give her to me," Serena said, throwing him a look of contempt. She took Louisa from him and held her tightly in her arms. At once some subtle magic that she possessed began to work, and the child who had cried so bitterly in her father's arms quietened into hiccups.

He saw his wife watching his discomfiture with cynical delight. "Be ready to leave in an hour," he told her curtly, and escaped.

His last memory of Serena was the farewells at the door. She kissed Dawn and hugged Louisa and seemed about to let him go without a glance. But at the last minute he saw her gazing at him, her eyes puzzled and distraught, as though she'd been struck by a thought that troubled and confused her. He gave her a brief nod and drove away.

Back in Rome he worked hard at not thinking about her. On her wedding day he went out onto the test track with the firm's newest model and drove it until he was exhausted. He told himself that was that, and now he could really forget her.

He bought Louisa the doll and was hurt at her lack of interest. But then Dawn took a "rest cure" at an expensive Swiss clinic that specialized in beauty treatments. He used her absence to repair his relationship with his daughter, and soon they were back on their old affectionate footing.

Life went on. Serena's name was never mentioned until the day, a month later, when Dawn said casually, "Serena called today. She's started a business course at the local college."

"That'll be a great help for running a hardware store," he observed ironically.

"Oh heavens, did I forget to tell you? The wedding was canceled. She practically stood Andrew up at the altar."

He was shaken by such a storm of unreasoning joy that he had to get away from her lest it show on his face. He knew it could make no possible difference to him whether she was married or not, yet his heart insisted on being lighter.

All that had been five years ago. Since then he'd had no word of Serena, nor had he spoken to her until today. Gradually he'd come to believe that he must have imagined that scorching moment of recognition when her soul had seemed to look directly into his.

His relationship with his wife had gone from bad to worse, until a few weeks ago, during their worst fight ever, Dawn had declared that their marriage was over.

"I want a divorce and a decent income," she'd snapped. "Then perhaps I can start to have some fun out of life."

"You can have everything you want as long as I get custody of Louisa," had been his immediate response.

"Oh no. Louisa stays with me. But you can see her now and then—when I think it's suitable."

"If I pick up the bills, you mean?" he said cynically.

"Forget it. I'm not having her living with the kind of dubious characters you find entertaining. There'll be a divorce all right, but she'll stay here, and the less she sees of you the better."

Next day she'd gone, taking Louisa. He'd had them traced to Milan, then Vienna, then Paris, but always Dawn managed to keep one jump ahead of his detectives. After Paris she'd vanished into thin air. He hadn't even known she was in England until half an hour ago.

Now everything was in turmoil. Dawn was dead, his child had disappeared, and he must face Serena again.

Two

Serena set down the receiver and sat for a long time, trying not to feel shaken by the sound of Carlo's voice. For years she'd resolutely sought to bar him from her thoughts, yet still that well-remembered resonant timbre had the power to disturb her. It was all wrong. This man was a bully who'd made both Dawn and Louisa miserable with his callous indifference to their feelings. She ought to hate him, not feel this terrible inner disturbance.

She looked up to find Celia, who'd answered the phone, watching her. "That was Louisa's father," she said.

Celia nodded. She was a middle-aged woman of few words and a great deal of kindly common sense. She'd worked for Serena's home-help agency from the day it was opened, and was a tower of strength. It was always Celia that Serena turned to when there was a really difficult job, and the one she must do now was the most difficult of all. "I gather he wants her back," she said.

"Yes, and he's not going to have her," Serena declared. "That poor little thing's suffered enough without him snatching her away now she's found some security."

"Of course, he *is* her father..." Celia mused. "Perhaps he loves her. Perhaps she loves him."

Serena hesitated. She liked Celia, but she couldn't reveal to her the shattering secret Dawn had entrusted to her. "You didn't meet him when he came over five years ago, did you?" she asked.

"No. I'm glad I didn't. The way you and Dawn have always spoken of him, he sounds quite terrible."

"He's certainly cold and unkind. The day he arrived I was walking in the wood with Louisa. She was having a lovely time, laughing and enjoying herself. Then she scampered away and when I caught up with her he was there, and all the joy had gone out of her face. If you could have seen the way she ran to me, as if she was scared of him."

"Does she ever mention him now?"

"No. Since her mother died she's barely said a word about anything. It breaks my heart to see her so quiet." She set her jaw in sudden determination. "Celia, I'm going to see that child smiling and happy again, I swear it. We can keep her safe from that man. Thank heavens she likes you so much. I want you to take her right away from here, today. There's no time to lose."

Celia looked alarmed, but there was no arguing with Serena when she spoke in that decisive tone. Five years had transformed her into a self-assured woman who ran her business efficiently, made up her mind and acted without delay. In a few minutes she was on the phone to a contact who dealt in rented holiday cottages. By early afternoon the three of them were on the road, Serena at the wheel of her car and Louisa sitting docilely in the back, with Celia's arm about her.

Their destination was Claverdon, a village in the midlands, about two hours' drive away. The cottage was small but comfortable, and luckily Louisa took to it at once. Serena bid her goodbye with a hug and a whispered promise, "It's going to be all right, darling." Louisa nodded back gravely, but didn't smile.

Serena headed back to London, where she'd lived for the past two years since her grandparents had died. As she drove, she reflected on what she was doing. Although Dawn had appointed her Louisa's guardian, she wasn't sure how that would stand up legally in the face of Carlo's opposition. She was probably breaking the law, but she was prepared to take that risk to protect the little girl she loved. Louisa was all she had left of Dawn.

Although they were cousins, she'd always regarded Dawn as her sister because they'd been brought up together after Serena's parents were killed in a car crash when she was six months old. Liz and Frank were already caring for ten-year-old Dawn, whose parents had divorced and gone on to other partners, and they willingly gave a home to the orphaned baby.

Dawn had dazzled her from the moment she became old enough to distinguish one person from another. Dawn was beautiful, clever and adventurous. At home and at school she broke the rules and did it with a dash and style that made her every action seem romantic and wonderful. Best of all, she allowed Serena to share in her thrilling escapades. When Dawn began dating boys that Liz and Frank considered unsuitable, it was little Serena who carried notes back and forth.

Then Dawn had left home in search of excitement.
For a year Serena had followed her progress across the
world through postcards, until the day she called to say
she'd married the young Italian racing driver, Carlo
Valetti, and was "divinely happy." At the impressionable age of thirteen, Serena had been thrilled. She'd
longed for the day when Dawn would invite her to visit
her splendid home in Rome, but the invitation had
never come, and the postcards, too, were fewer. She refused to believe that her idol had forgotten her. Dawn
was just very busy with her new life.

And then she'd returned to England. She was reti-
cent about her marriage, and Serena had realized she
was unhappy but didn't want to criticize her husband.
Her charm had been as dazzling as ever, and Serena had
fallen once more under her spell.

Carlo's arrival had been a shock. He was at once the
most disagreeable and the most attractive man she'd
ever met. His lean good looks and dark eyes had caused
a sudden disquieting tension about her heart at the first
meeting. But he'd dispelled that by growling at her.

For a while at the dance, he'd seemed more likable.
His burst of spontaneous laughter had transformed
him, smoothing out lines of worry that had touched his
face too soon for a man in his twenties. When they
waltzed, the feeling of his strong arms had caused a
treacherous excitement to stir in her. She'd resolved not
to dance with him again, and then been disappointed
when he didn't ask her.

It had been a secret relief when her fiancé returned.
Dear, solid Andrew had been her closest friend for
years, and everyone had taken it for granted they would
marry. She was happy and comfortable in the thought,
but now all her comfort was destroyed. Carlo evidently

regarded him as a bumpkin and couldn't speak to him without a touch of sarcasm that roused Serena's indignation.

Her cheeks still burned when she remembered Carlo's look of contempt when he saw her in her wedding dress. It had been even worse to overhear Patricia ask if he didn't think she looked wonderful, and to hear his coldly scornful reply.

Was that when this sophisticated, cosmopolitan man decided that he couldn't be bothered with a provincial wedding? Serena could forgive him for insulting her, but not for ignoring Louisa's tearful pleas to be allowed to stay.

In a fury, she'd confronted him and found herself facing an ice wall. Carlo had made up his mind and that was that.

But there was another memory that refused to fade, and that hinted maybe everything wasn't so simple: for a shattering moment his hand had burned her arm, and his eyes—suddenly naked and defenseless—had looked into hers. In that instant she'd felt that her own heart, too, was naked, letting him read the treacherous thoughts and sensations that troubled her. Appalled, she'd wrenched herself away and fled, not only from him but from the incredible suspicion that flashed through her brain.

When he'd gone she persuaded herself that she'd imagined the whole thing. Only the lingering consciousness in her flesh, where he'd touched her, made a mockery of her reasoning.

To her horror she found that she couldn't bear to be near Andrew. He'd been bewildered at her wild insistence that the wedding must be postponed, but he'd fallen meekly in with her wishes, both then and later when it was canceled altogether.

She smiled fondly at the thought of Andrew, now happily married to Patricia, with their third baby on the way. Carlo had been right about them. How strange that such an unfeeling man had been the one to see the truth!

She'd gone to business college, and then set up her own home-help agency. It had flourished so well that she'd moved to London and expanded. It was her boast that she could find the right person for any job, and her satisfied customers included several titles and one minor royalty.

Her success was measured in the small, elegant apartment in the heart of London, and the glossy car she was driving now. The car was the one extravagant note in her well-ordered life, costing more than she could afford, and giving her a delightful sense of guilty pleasure. It wasn't, unfortunately, the very best of its kind. The state of the art was the sleek, beautiful Valetti X7. That was way beyond her purse, and besides, she wasn't going to swell Carlo's coffers—but she scoured the motoring magazines for the first hint of the new model.

She was still unmarried after several promising romances had fizzled out. She told herself that she was being cautious lest she repeat Dawn's experience; but then Carlo's face would come before her inner eye again, full of that look of scorching intensity, and she would shut off her thoughts quickly, before they strayed into forbidden territory.

A few short weeks ago Dawn and Louisa had fled back to England. "I had to come," Dawn had said desperately. "Carlo wants to divorce me and keep Louisa."

Serena was appalled. "Even Carlo wouldn't do that, surely?"

"You don't know what he'd do," Dawn said bitterly. "To him, Louisa is just another piece of property, and Carlo never lets go of property."

"Then we'll fight him with his own weapons."

They'd consulted the best lawyer in the business. At his suggestion Dawn made a new will, appointing Serena her child's guardian in case of her death. "Just in case..." he'd said, and Dawn had signed, laughing at the precaution that would never be needed.

But in a tragically short time it had become reality. Dawn had started a feverish cold, which she'd refused to take seriously. "I'm going to a party," she'd insisted. "It's years since I've enjoyed myself, and I'm going to have fun tonight. Look after Louisa for me, won't you?"

"Of course, but I wish you wouldn't go. You're so flushed."

"I'll be fine."

In the early hours she'd crept home, shivering violently. Serena had called the doctor, and within an hour Dawn was in hospital. Even then Serena wasn't too worried. People didn't die from pneumonia these days. But without warning, Dawn had a heart attack. Serena sat by her bed, holding her hand and knowing it was for the last time.

"Serena..." Dawn had whispered her name. "Come near—something I must tell you."

Fighting back her grief, Serena leaned close. Dawn seemed to fight for strength, and at last she managed to say, "Louisa...take care of her."

"Of course," Serena promised through her tears.

"She's not . . . Carlo's child."

Serena stared. "Not Carlo's?"

"I couldn't help it. Don't . . . blame me."

Serena shook her head. "Does Carlo know?"

"No," Dawn whispered, "but he has no right to her . . . remember that," she whispered.

"Dawn, who was her real father?"

Dawn took a painful breath and tried to speak, but no sound emerged. All at once the last of her strength ran out and she closed her eyes. An hour later she died.

In her secret soul Serena was a little shocked at the discovery that Dawn had betrayed her husband. Her own fiercely honorable nature would have made it impossible for her to do such a thing. She would have left a man rather than deceive him. But she dismissed the thought as soon as she had it. It seemed cruel to judge Dawn when she was no longer there to explain what had driven her to act so out-of-character. Who could know what Carlo had done to his wife? Serena's grief made it easy to transfer the blame to him.

But for the moment she couldn't indulge that grief. There was work to be done. She had only Louisa left. She'd promised to protect her, and she'd keep that vow whatever it cost.

Dawn's funeral took place in the village of Delmer on a cold, drizzly day, and the atmosphere accorded with Serena's mood. She was on edge all through the service, looking for Carlo, but there was no sign of him. Cynically she decided that, despite his fine words, he was probably occupied with a business deal.

But when she turned to leave the church, she saw him standing at the back, plainly having come in quietly after the service started. He looked at her, meeting her eyes with a challenge, and stepped forward to intercept her as soon as she was out of the church. "Where's Louisa?" he demanded without preamble.

"I thought it would upset her to be here today."

"I asked you where she *is*."

"Safe."

A look of fury flickered across his face and vanished as if he'd driven it away by sheer force. "I want to see her," he said firmly.

"I'm afraid that's impossible. I promised Dawn."

"You're doing something very dangerous," he said in a hard voice. "I won't tolerate your interference."

"Don't start telling me what you will and won't tolerate," she said angrily. "Louisa is staying with me, where her mother wanted her to be."

She turned aside, to get around him, but he seized her arm, saying angrily, "Now look . . ."

At once two burly men, who'd moved up quietly to stand behind Carlo, took hold of him and forced him to release Serena. "I came prepared," she explained, nodding to the men, so that they stood back.

He gave a scornful laugh. "A bodyguard? How melodramatic!"

"I remember your methods of getting your own way."

Before he could answer, there was a slight touch on his arm and he turned to find Mrs. Brady, the vicar's wife he'd collided with on that summer evening that seemed like an age ago. "I'm so glad to see you again," she said kindly, "although I don't suppose you remember me."

"I remember our meeting with great pleasure," he said courteously.

"We were all so fond of Dawn. But let's not stand in the rain. We can talk some more at the reception."

"I should like that," Carlo replied, seeing Serena's start of dismay out of the corner of one eye. "Perhaps I can give you and your husband a lift there."

"That's very kind. I'll just tell Bill."

She bustled away, leaving Carlo and Serena confronting each other. "I almost believe you weren't going to invite me," he said. "Will you tell me where the reception is, or must I ask the Bradys?"

"It's at the house," she said stiffly. "And you're wasting your time. Louisa isn't there."

His eyes narrowed. "Do you understand your own presumption?"

"Yes, I've presumed to claim your 'property.'" Serena said ironically. "Only she's not property, she's a child with feelings, and she's not going to be hurt by seeing us fight over her."

Carlo turned and walked away without a word. He was afraid of letting his angry frustration overcome him. He already felt he was fighting on shifting ground. The sight of her had given him a shock. She was so different from what he remembered. The young, half-wild creature had given way to this cool, sophisticated woman. Instead of the soft, untidy hair that had danced delightfully about her face, she was now sleekly groomed, with every strand pinned in place. And to his dismay, her worldly sheen intensified her slight facial resemblance to Dawn.

He moved mechanically through the reception, saying what was expected of him, but always conscious of Serena out of the corner of his eye. Eventually he noticed that she had gone, and after a moment he found her in the garden, sitting on a rustic bench. Despite her expensive black dress and perfect coiffure, she no longer looked glossily aloof. She looked lonely and disconsolate, and suddenly it was easy to speak to her. "You shouldn't sit out here," he said. "It's cold and damp."

"I can't bear it in there," she said with a sigh. "They all talk so—on and on. There's no peace."

"I know." He sat down beside her. She half turned her face and he could see that she'd been crying, but she wiped the evidence away at once. "Don't do that," he said. "Why shouldn't you cry? Or is it because I'm here? Do you think I haven't grieved?"

"Have you?" she asked, wonderingly.

"Of course. Not for the loss of my wife, for I lost her years ago. But for the way things once were, and the marriage we might have had if—" He checked himself. This wasn't the moment to speak of Dawn's greed and selfishness. "If things hadn't gone wrong," he finished lamely. "When something ends, you always wonder if you could have done better. If I'd been older—I don't know—perhaps I would have been less dazzled by her, and if I'd been less dazzled I might have—managed better."

"She was dazzling, wasn't she?" Serena said eagerly. "When I was a child, if she let me do things for her, I was in heaven."

"Yes," he murmured wryly, "she could be delightful when you did what she wanted. How old were you when she left?"

"About twelve."

He nodded as she confirmed his suspicion. Serena had known her cousin as an impressionable child, and for only a few weeks as an adult. She'd never had a chance to learn her true character.

"I don't see your grandparents anywhere," he observed.

"They died two years ago, within a few days of each other. She went first, and he just faded away. They're buried together."

"They loved each other very much," Carlo said, almost to himself.

"Yes they did. I was glad for them that it happened that way, and neither of them had to drag out an unhappy life without the other."

"I'm glad for them, too. They struck me as very much a part of each other. But I wish I'd known. I'd have sent flowers—or even come to the funeral if you'd let me. Why are you staring at me like that?"

"I was thinking what a short memory you have," she said coldly. "Dawn wanted to come to the funeral, but you kept her in Italy to entertain some business associates. She was in tears on the phone."

"I imagine she was," he said dryly. "Dawn was very good at being tearful on the phone when she wanted to get out of an irksome duty."

"Don't slander her," she cried.

"Serena, I swear to you that I never heard about your grandparents, and I never prevented Dawn from coming to their funeral. I wouldn't have done that. And while we're setting the record straight, I never threatened to throw her out. Divorce was her idea, not mine. She was going to keep Louisa and let me see her only when it suited her, which would have meant never. I told her I preferred it the other way around."

"That's not the way she made it sound."

"I can only tell you the way it was. I can't force you to believe me."

She rose. "I must go back to my guests."

"I won't come in again," he said. "It's time I went. Take good care of my child."

"Did you think you needed to tell me that?" she asked sharply.

"I don't know what I need to tell you. I don't understand a woman who hides a child from her father and imagines she's doing right. You'll be hearing from me."

He shook her hand briefly and walked through the garden until he reached the road where his car was parked. As he drove away he looked in his rearview mirror. Another car parked unobtrusively nearby, started up and followed him, and he gave a grunt of satisfaction. After a quarter of a mile he stopped in a lay-by and got out to wait while the other car halted too. The driver, a nondescript man called Banyon, approached him. "Did you see everything you needed?" Carlo asked curtly.

"I took a good look at Miss Fletcher, like you told me," Banyon said. "There was no sign of the little girl."

"No. I half expected that. So, she's hidden my daughter, and it's your job to find her."

Banyon shook his head. "It won't be easy."

"Just do whatever you have to," Carlo ordered him. "Keep that young woman under surveillance night and day. I want to know everything she does, everywhere she goes. Tap her phone if you must. I hired you because you're supposed to be one of the best investigators in the business."

"*The* best," Banyon insisted.

"Prove it by finding my daughter," Carlo snapped. Then he got back into his car and drove away.

Three

The doorbell rang while Serena was in the shower. She called out for her visitor to wait, while she hurriedly dried off and flung on her robe. "You're early," she began to say as she pulled open the door.

"May I come in?" Carlo asked.

She had a sudden conviction that she wasn't properly covered, and stepped hastily back. He followed her inside her apartment. "I'm sorry I'm not whoever you're expecting," he said.

She refused to answer. Whoever she was expecting was none of his business. "I'll be with you in a moment," she said, and hurried into her bedroom to dress. When she returned he was standing by the mantelpiece, holding a picture of Dawn and Louisa that had been standing there. His expression was one she'd never expected to see. There was despairing sadness in it, but

also a kind of subtle delight, as though the picture reminded him of a joy too great to be quite extinguished.

"Carlo..." she said uncertainly.

He looked up sharply, and the expression vanished in
a flash, to be replaced by a blank mask. "You've cut her
hair," he accused.

"Louisa wanted it cut," Serena explained.

"That's impossible. She loved having long hair."

"You mean you loved it. She hated having to spend
time on it in the morning, so Dawn took her to a hair-
dresser and he cut it short."

"She looks like a boy," Carlo said, outraged.

"Well, she *is* a bit of a tomboy at heart. I promise
you, Louisa loves it short. That's why I took a picture
of her."

"But she looks so different," he mused, studying the
picture again. "I don't know her like this."

For a moment he sounded almost forlorn, Serena
thought, but she pushed the idea aside. She couldn't
afford to start feeling sorry for him. He'd already made
her uneasy. His denial of things Dawn had told her had
troubled her more than she wanted to admit, and his
remark that Dawn "was good at being tearful on the
phone" had brought back a memory: Dawn, a beautiful sought-after teenager, wriggling out of a date with
a dull boy because a more glamorous one had come
along. She'd called him up and spun him a sad tale
about how she had just had to stay at home and look
after her "sick little cousin Serena," while the cousin
herself had listened, doubled up with laughter.

Of course, that was entirely different, she told herself, a piece of teenage foolery that many girls indulged
in. But the memory remained.

Carlo sighed. "I came to ask you what became of my wife's things—I mean, the small, personal possessions."

"They're still here."

"May I have them?"

The request took her aback. For some reason, she hadn't thought Carlo would bother. "I've put them all together," she said in a gentler tone. "It's through here."

She led him into the spare bedroom where Dawn and Louisa had slept, and opened a drawer containing Dawn's driving license, wallet and other items from her purse. She left them with him and went into the kitchen. When he returned she had coffee ready. "I suppose you're surprised to see me," he remarked.

"No, I'm more surprised at not having heard anything from you these past few days."

"I haven't gone away, and I won't. But I don't want to be constantly fighting you. We both love Louisa and I want what's best for her. Tell me how she is."

"She's fine, I promise you. She's being well looked after, by someone she likes."

He was silent for a moment, before saying, "We didn't have much chance to talk after the funeral. Will you tell me what happened to Dawn? Why did she die?"

"She had the flu, but she wouldn't take care of it. She went to a party, and when she came home she was much worse. I rushed her to the hospital and they said she had pneumonia. She started to recover, but then she had a heart attack."

He sighed and said with a touch of irony, "She could never resist a party. I'm not sure what she was looking for, but she always thought she could find it at the next party, in the next bottle of champagne, or the next boyfriend.'' He saw Serena's lip curl and added, ''Our marriage was over a long time ago, by her choice. After that—'' he shrugged ''—sometimes she was discreet, sometimes she didn't bother. I didn't admire her taste in men.''

''Neither did I,'' Serena said coldly, looking pointedly at him.

''I won't pretend not to understand you. Dawn and I should never have married, but we did, and I don't walk out on my contracts. When I've given my word, I keep it, even when it involves a loss.''

''Dawn was a human being, not a contract,'' Serena protested.

''But a marriage is a contract,'' he pointed out. ''And surely human contracts should be kept with even more honor than we'd show for the business kind? As a businesswoman—and as a woman—I'm sure you agree.''

She agreed so completely that for a moment she was left nonplussed. It annoyed her to find herself in accord with him, especially as she now knew that Dawn's attitude to human contracts hadn't been above reproach. But Dawn had been driven beyond endurance, she reminded herself quickly.

''I do agree,'' she said, ''but I think people need more than honor. They need warmth and love.''

''And you think I fail in those things? You presume too much. You know nothing about me. And it is you, not I, who is depriving Louisa of her father's love this minute.''

She refused to rise to the bait. ''We're getting off the subject,'' she said. ''Is there anything else you want?''

''Yes. Who was with her when she died?''

''I was.''

His face softened. "And that was hard for you, because you loved her, didn't you?"

"Yes," she said shortly. She was wary of his sympathy.

"Was she conscious?"

"Most of the time."

"And did she—speak of me?"

Serena hesitated, feeling herself in a quandary. At last she said simply, "Yes."

"What did she say?"

"I'm sorry, I can't tell you."

"Can't, or won't?"

"Whichever you prefer."

There was a ring at the doorbell. Serena hurried to answer, and found Julia Henly, her assistant, standing outside, clutching the firm's account books. "Sorry I'm a bit late," Julia said, entering. "Oh, I'm sorry." She stopped as she saw Carlo. "Do you want the figures another time?"

"No, we'll stick to our arrangement," Serena said crisply. "Signor Valetti is just leaving.'

Carlo picked up the photograph from the mantelpiece. "May I keep this?" he asked.

"Of course." Serena knew a moment's pity for him now that the picture was all he had, and this time she didn't try to overcome it.

"Thank you." He slipped the picture out of its frame and put it into his briefcase. He gave Julia a courteous nod and went out into the hall. "Serena, this is all wrong. We're the two people who love Louisa the most, and we shouldn't be fighting. She needs love from both of us. Please, won't you reconsider what you're doing?"

Serena's face was sad, but there was no hesitation in her answer. "I'm sorry, Carlo. I have a promise to keep."

"Very well, if that's your decision. I tried. I can do no more."

He saw the quick frown that came to her face as she divined the hint of threat in the final words. But she said nothing, only faced him with her head up. He walked away down the stairs, resisting the temptation to look back and see if she was watching him with the same troubled look. If she was, it was better not to know. He'd given her every chance, and what happened now was on her head.

In the parking lot he walked past his own car to the one beyond, and got in. Banyon, who was sitting in the driver's seat, said, "Did you get what you went for?"

"That and more." Carlo thrust his hand into the brown envelope, and pulled out Dawn's passport, which he flicked open, revealing that it was Louisa's passport too.

"Will you be able to use that?" Banyon asked.

"No, but I can get my daughter a separate passport from the Italian consulate if I hand this in first. There's also this." He showed Banyon the picture. "She looks different with her hair so short."

"Yes, she does, doesn't she?" Banyon mused, comparing the pictures with one he took from his pocket. "I might have missed her if I'd still been going by the old one you gave me." He grinned. "And Miss Fletcher just gave you all this, for the asking?"

"Yes."

"She's not so bright after all, is she?"

"She's bright enough," Carlo said slowly. "It's just that . . . she wasn't suspicious."

"More the fool, then. She should have known you were going to pull a fast one."

"Yes," Carlo said harshly. "But she didn't."

He got out, slamming the door behind him and went to his own car. He told himself that he'd done a good thing, a clever, shrewd thing. But his heart didn't believe it. He'd seen the genuine pity in her eyes, and he knew it was that pity that had robbed her of caution, helping him to "pull a fast one." All the way back to his hotel he reminded himself that he was in the right, that this was war, with no quarter given. But he felt like a wretch.

In the lonely, waiting days that followed, Carlo found himself haunted by the thought of Liz and Frank. That two people should love each other so deeply that one couldn't survive without the other served to underline the emptiness of his own life. One day, driven by an irresistible impulse, he got into his car and drove a hundred miles to Delmer. He bought flowers in the village and took them to the churchyard.

It was raining when he arrived, a gentle, English spring shower that touched him lightly. It took him only a few moments to find where Liz and Frank lay together. There was a small urn on the grave, with some fresh flowers already in it, as if someone had been there already that day. He laid his bouquet down and rose, looking around, half hoping, and at last he saw Serena, standing a few yards away, watching him.

"I don't understand," she said as he came up to her.

"Try to believe that I'm not a monster, and it's really very simple," he said. He felt awkward, but when he looked into her eyes he saw that there was no hostility in them, and that reassured him. "I didn't know you'd be here."

"I come every few weeks to check on the house. I was just going there, if you'd like some coffee."

"Thank you."

He followed her car in his own, noting with half his mind that she'd bought an expensive model, built for speed, a car that only a connoisseur would choose. He drew up behind her outside the house and they raced the last few yards through the driving rain. "This is probably the last time I'll be here," she said when she let him into the house. "I'm going to sell this place."

"But you can't!" The words jerked out, scandalized.

"I can't live here. My home is in London. Besides," she sighed, "it makes me too sad to come back. I was happy here as a child, and now I can't bear the emptiness."

"You were happy because you were loved," he said. "Your grandparents had so much love themselves that it overflowed on you."

He sensed that he'd taken her aback. "That's exactly how it was. Did Dawn tell you?"

"No, she never told me anything about her earlier life. But I met your grandparents. I know that's how it must have been."

She stared at him as if trying to reconcile this empathy with her image of him. But she turned away without saying anything, and began to go through the house, drawing the curtains aside and letting in some light. He watched her, entranced by the way she moved, the graceful swaying of her slender frame that was like reeds rippling with the water.

She was casually dressed in jeans and sweater, and nature had blessed her with a figure that suited them perfectly—neat, small-boned and without pronounced curves. But despite her lack of voluptuousness, Carlo found everything about her deeply feminine, from the soft, warm tones of her voice to the long lines of her neck. He ached for her. Part of him hated her for what she was doing to him, and yet he ached to touch her and see her smile in response.

She paused, looking out the French window to where the garden lay under rain. "You were right," she said quietly. "I was so happy here. I didn't realize just how happy until it was all over. We had such wonderful adventures in that wood."

"We? You and Dawn?"

"No, she was too much older than me for that. There was a little gang of village children who used to come here, and we'd play Cavaliers and Roundheads. Andrew used to borrow pots and pans from his father's shop to make the helmets, but we stopped that after one of them got dented, and we had to pay for it out of our pocket money."

He grinned. "I'll wager you were the gang leader."

"Yes, I was the bossy one," she said with a laugh. "But I was the daring one, too. I used to paddle in the stream when it was too cold for the others, and climb the highest trees. Andrew challenged me to a tree-climbing contest once, but he got giddy halfway up and I had to rescue him."

"I can imagine. He hasn't changed. I saw him with Patricia at the funeral, and today in the village. I noticed how his hardware shop had been transformed. Don't tell me he's the brain behind that."

Serena smiled. "No, it was her work. You were right about them. And of course, he *was* just the same then. I can see it now."

Carlo grew suddenly serious again. "I could almost be glad to leave Louisa with you if you could give her the kind of childhood you had—playing 'let's pretend' with other children, climbing trees and paddling in streams, learning about nature, and developing her own personality." Serena looked at him curiously, but he went on, as if only half aware of her. "She had a brief taste of it the first time she was here. She was so happy."

"Then why did you take her away?"

"Because I had to."

"Oh yes, because there was a crisis." She added wryly, "Except that there was no crisis."

He met her eyes. "I think you know better than that—don't you?"

He'd caught her off guard, and for a moment the truth was there in her eyes, as it had been once in the past. She checked herself, but he'd seen it. "How could I know?" she asked slowly.

"Because you're a woman, with a woman's heart and understanding. You didn't see it then, you were too inexperienced. But Serena, are you going to tell me that at some moment in the past few years, you didn't understand why I ran away?"

She took a deep ragged breath. "I don't know what you—"

"Don't lie," he said with sudden passionate urgency. "Don't hide from it. I ran away from *you,* and you know it. I ran to preserve my honor—and yours. I was married to your cousin, and that marriage bound me, not with love but with obligation." He faced her.

"I ran for the same reason that you jilted your fiancé," he said deliberately.

The color that rose in her face was the same color of wild roses he'd seen there before, on the day they first met. The look in her eyes was full of confusion. "I canceled my wedding because I realized in time that I wasn't the right wife for Andrew," she said cautiously. "But that was all."

"Was it—all?"

She looked at him, and drew her breath as if to speak. His heart beat with anticipation. But the next moment a piercing beep tore through the air between them. Serena started and looked as though she'd been awakened out of a dream. "What's that?" she demanded.

Cursing, Carlo shut off the alarm of his wristwatch. "I set it to remind me to make a call," he said furiously.

She moved away from him as if seeking an escape. Her voice was slightly breathless. "I'm afraid the phone here's disconnected."

"It doesn't matter. I have one with me."

"You'd better make the call then. I'm sure it's urgent."

The spell was broken. Furiously he went out to the car and snatched up the portable to dial his office. But the line refused to connect. He returned to the house, dialing again. This time he managed to reach the works in Rome, and asked to speak to Capriati, his assistant, whom he'd left in charge. But although Capriati had been warned to expect the call, he was out.

Carlo shrugged and hung up. The man's inefficiency faded to nothing beside the absorbing sight of Serena gracefully opening windows in the back room. When she threw open the French doors, he set the phone down on the hall table and went to stand beside her, looking out over the garden. "You mustn't sell it," he urged. "You can't sell anything so beautiful. It might fall into the hands of people who wouldn't love it properly."

She turned wondering eyes on him. "You feel that, too?"

He wanted to say that he could see into her heart, but it was too soon, and he wasn't quite sure. He followed her down the few steps on the lawn. The rain had stopped, and the sun was beginning to come out, turning the droplets on the trees to diamonds. "It's just as I remember from the first time I came here," he said quietly. "There's the hammock, and there's the little wood with the break in the trees. Louisa came running to me over the grass, and a moment later you appeared...."

He felt caught up in a dream. She had been so beautiful, drifting through the trees like a vision—an unlikely vision with bare feet, torn jeans and tousled hair, natural and utterly enchanting. "But everything was in bloom then," he said slowly, "not bare as it is now."

She spoke in the same quiet tone, as though the dream had touched her, too. "The bareness is passing," she said. "You can already see the buds, soon the blossoms will be out and it will be summer again."

"But not like that summer," he said softly.

She met his eyes. "No," she whispered, "not like that summer."

A lock of silky hair came free and fell down the side of her face. As he'd done once before, he reached out to take it and pin it back. But no sooner had his fingers brushed against her cheek than he became absolutely still. His heart was beating madly, loud enough to be heard, yet not loudly enough to mask the urgent sound of her breath coming through parted lips. Her eyes were wide and fixed on him, as his were on her. Together they were the unmoving axis of a universe that whirled about them, flinging stars in all directions, hurling planets into space. There was one blinding moment when they saw it all, when everything that had happened in the intervening years made sudden sense. The next instant she was in his arms.

And then it was all mad intoxication as he sensed the sweetness of wild honey on his lips, and spring breezes in his nostrils. In the first moment she stiffened in instinctive protest, but then, as if recognising an irresistible truth, she let herself go, melting into his embrace as if she'd been waiting for this one kiss. The sensation of her yielding to him drove Carlo to madness. For five years he'd fought his longing for her, lain awake through long, fevered nights, aching to see her slow smile, hear her husky voice and feel her naked flesh against his.

"Serena," he said hoarsely, "Serena...you know, don't you?"

"Yes," she could hardly whisper the word. "Yes...yes...."

He smothered her mouth with his own and felt the eagerness in her soft lips. It seemed like the first kiss he'd ever known, and in some ways, it was: the first kiss with the perfect woman, who'd been created for him and for whom he'd been created, the woman he'd thought could never be his. He wanted to kiss her and be kissed by her forever. He wanted far more than kisses, more than physical pleasure. He wanted the delight of the heart that only she could give.

He looked down on her, cupping her face in his hands. "What's happening to me," she whispered. "I didn't know this was going to happen, and yet—"

"And yet it had to happen," he finished for her. "Neither of us has planned anything, right from the start. We were taken over by powers outside our control. There was nothing we could do about it."

"I tried to pretend—I wanted to be strong—"

A few drops of moisture fell onto her face from the branches above them. They reminded him of tears, and he hastened to kiss them away. The knowledge that he hadn't been dreaming his dream alone pierced him with joy. "I, too, tried to be strong," he murmured. "If you knew how hard I fought you... but I have no strength left... I can't fight any more... can you?"

She shook her head dumbly. She seemed to be in a trance. Carlo laid his mouth on hers again, reveling in the soft curves of her lips. How often had they tempted him with what he couldn't have? And now he claimed possession and found them sweet and welcoming. She gave a little contented sigh, sending her warm breath into his mouth where it mingled with his own, inviting him, making his heart beat more strongly.

His body was pervaded with desire for her. All the strength in his arms was useless unless they held her close to him. His mouth was made only to kiss her, and every word it had ever uttered had been a waste of time. His whole being was concentrated in the need to lay his flesh against hers, to claim her and be united with her. But even stronger than the hunger of the flesh was the hunger of the heart. Where there had been loneliness, she'd created wonder, and only she could turn that wonder into glory.

The wind stirred the trees above them, making more glittering droplets shower down on them. They laughed and shook themselves free, but almost at once the laughter died and they looked at each other in awed silence. Gently, almost reverently, Carlo stroked her face.

"Come," he whispered. "Come... beloved."

Four

The bedroom was in shadow. Curtains covered the window, and the dusk of late afternoon was falling. It had been Serena's room when she lived here, and the bed was narrower than a double, but wider than a single: the perfect size for two people who wanted to be close.

As soon as Carlo had shut the door they clung together, not even kissing, but burying their faces in each other's warmth, as though sharing some mutual fear, perhaps the dread that after all this time it might prove an illusion. But then they drew apart, exchanging looks full of recognition, both knowing that it was real and there was nothing to fear.

He unbuttoned her blouse with fingers that shook with eagerness like an untried boy's. She made it easier for him by working on his own buttons, so that they were ready to throw their clothes aside at the same moment. He discovered that she wore no bra. Her breasts were small and firm, yet with a roundness that was infinitely enticing, and he surveyed her with pleasure. Everything about her delighted him, from the delicacy of her build to the revelations of desire in her rosy nipples. He caressed them lovingly and sensed the frisson that went through her.

She began to run her fingers through the dark, curly hair of his chest, and forks of lightning went through him. He groaned, fighting for control. He wanted her in every way a man could want a woman, but not yet. He couldn't risk losing his miracle by rushing it. They must reveal themselves gradually, exploring the gifts of each other by slow degrees, establishing trust before there could be abandon, tenderness before passion. So he tried to ignore the fire she'd ignited in his loins, and concentrated instead on the intriguing little smile that touched her lips as she explored his chest.

"I wondered..." she whispered, curling a strand of hair around one finger. "I often wondered if you were hairy or smooth-chested."

Her smile had already told him that. He wondered if she could read him as easily, detecting the almost gloating possessiveness of a man who'd discovered treasure, and was determined not to lose it again. "Did you have any preferences?" he asked softly.

She shook her head. "No, it was just one of the things that made you such a mystery to me."

"There was no mystery. I was simply afraid of you— and of myself. Now I don't have to be afraid anymore. I used to long for the right to do this..." As he spoke he was pulling at the pins in her hair, until it fell over his fingers. "*Serena,*" he whispered violently, and smothered her mouth.

She opened for him at once, taking his tongue deep into her, offering up the dark warmth inside to his exploration. As the tip of his tongue flickered against the silky smoothness of her skin, she made little sounds of pleasure that thrilled him. Her arms went trustingly about his neck and he pulled her closer, feeling the hardness of her nipples pressed to his chest. The knowledge of her desire for him was so wonderful that he groaned helplessly against her mouth.

At last they drew apart and stood looking at each other, their breasts rising and falling with the urgency of what had overtaken them. It was too late now for thought. They had come this far and there was no turning back. She took a step away from him toward the bed, but her eyes still held him as though by a silken cord, and he had no choice but to follow. She continued to move, and he to follow, until they reached the bed and he drew her into his arms again, pressing her down until they were lying together.

He kissed her mouth, her jaw, the length of her neck, laying his lips in the hollow at the base and reveling in her soft, sweet-smelling skin. An irresistible power drew him farther down to caress her breasts, teasing the nipples with his mouth. Above his head he heard her sigh, and felt the convulsions go through her body at every movement of his tongue.

Her sigh became whispered words. "Carlo... Carlo...*yes*."

Some new note in her voice galvanized him into action, making him throw off the rest of his clothes. She followed his lead, working at the zip of her jeans, but it was he who pulled them off, then the panties. He was in a fever to hold her nakedness against his own. She seemed so slight against his big frame, but there was strength in her embrace and purpose in the innocently wanton way she offered herself to him. The afternoon light coming through the curtains was strong enough to reveal them to each other, but to his joy she showed no hint of shyness. She seemed to revel in letting him see her, as if she knew that she was beautiful, and he paid tribute to her beauty with lips and tongue, arms and hands.

She writhed feverishly in his arms, guiding him with instinctive sensuality to bestow those caresses that pleased her most, until at last she drew him over herself in a gesture that was half a plea, half a demand. His manhood was hard and eager, seeking its way into her, feeling the hot, moist readiness that welcomed it home. A shaft of agonizing pleasure shot through him as he was enfolded in her intimate embrace. Her thighs were warm and insistent about his hips, releasing him only to draw him back, half-fearful lest the glory be snatched away.

The pleasure was driving him to the point of madness, but greater than pleasure was the happiness of knowing that she truly wanted him. She revealed that in the warmth of her glowing skin, the sensual, provocative movements by which she enticed him on, and the brilliance of her eyes gazing up at him. He watched her face, almost worshipping her for what she was giving him.

The sound of her breathing was coming faster, or it might have been his own. He couldn't tell. They were one. He only knew that as his moment came her voice mingled with his in a cry of ecstasy, and they clung together as though suddenly seeing some danger that could only be faced in each other's arms.

At last the tumult died. His heartbeat slowed and he found himself lying with his head on her breast. He knew he'd passed a turning point in his life. Nothing would ever be the same again. This was his woman, who *had* to belong to him. He'd thought himself a civilized man, but the feeling that possessed him was ancient, primitive and deadly. His ancestors, who'd lived with knives at the ready and fought and died for honor, would have understood it. He had claimed this woman, and she had claimed him. Now there was no other choice for either of them.

They fell asleep, locked in each other's arms and lay without moving, as though stunned by the completeness of their mutual possession. At last Carlo awoke, realizing that darkness had fallen and he must have slept for hours. It was the first time he'd slept properly since coming to England, but Serena's loving seemed to have driven all strain from him.

He discovered her gone, and looked up quickly to find her standing by the window, her body outlined by the moonlight, looking out onto the garden. He lay still, adoring so much beauty, then came and stood behind her, wrapping her in his arms and gazing over her shoulder at the place where they had discovered each other that afternoon. Now it seemed illuminated with new significance, as though they had just learned the true meaning of everything in the world. And this thought was shared between them without a word being spoken.

She let her head fall back against him, looking up as far as she could, so that her long, beautiful neck was bathed in moonlight. He leaned down to kiss it, feeling the cool skin beneath his fevered lips. "I was afraid I'd find you gone," he murmured."

"Never," she whispered. "I'll never leave you."

As soon as she'd said the words a startled look came into her eyes, as though a stranger's voice had echoed through her. He spoke quickly before she could retract. "Promise me," he urged.

"I don't know what I—"

"Promise me."

No sound emerged, but her lips shaped the word "yes" and he was content. He became absorbed in the sight of her naked body turned to silver in the ghostly light, and began to trace patterns on the smooth skin with his fingers, watching the play of shadows. She leaned back against him and slipped her hands behind her to glide the length of his thighs. Carlo could feel her breathing becoming deeper as he moved closer to her breasts, until at last he cupped them, each one so small and delicate that he could hold it easily. He touched the nipples subtly, loving them with gentle caresses that made her sigh.

He turned her in his arms and kissed her deeply. Desire was pulsing through him again, answering her own desire that he could sense leaping through her slim body. Every urgent movement she made seemed to be a reaffirmation of her promise to him. Suddenly the warmth that engulfed him was not only of the flesh but of the heart, as though her wholehearted giving was beating back the loneliness of all his life. When he drew her down again onto the bed, he was seeking far more than physical pleasure. This woman could unlock doors and light up the world for him. She possessed a secret, and without it his life would never be whole again.

The first time had been a discovery; the second was a confirmation and a promise of infinite delights to come in the long vista of the future. He loved her slowly, savoring the sensation of being inside her and the shocks of ecstasy that shivered through him. Her eager responsiveness raised him to the level of the gods, making him return her gifts a thousandfold. The final explosion left him more at peace than he had ever been before in his life. The moment when he slipped over the edge into sleep was no more than a continuation of that peace.

Carlo opened his eyes to find the dawn creeping through the curtains. Serena was curled up beside him, her soft breath warming his skin. He eased an arm about her, trying not to awaken her, and she snuggled in still farther, burying her face against him in a way that tugged at his heart.

He was still partly asleep, caught in that pearly gray time of shadows, when what had seemed to be reality dissolved into nothing, and vague, unfocused outlines hardened into a new reality. He had a sensation that every path in his life had converged on this moment.

There in the shadows was his father, Emilio, whom he'd been raised to revere rather than love. He'd strived to fulfill Papa's expectations, while knowing it was impossible. Emilio had been a cold, vain man, who'd always made his son feel second best.

His mother was there in the shadows, too: beautiful, warmhearted and well-meaning, but lacking courage. She'd loved her son, but even for his sake she couldn't endure her husband's chilly self-obsession, and when Carlo was twelve she had run away. She'd left a note, begging her son's forgiveness, which the weeping boy had torn up.

Her departure had left a loveless void in his life. As he grew up he tried to fill it by emulating his father's achievements on the racetrack. He'd been a brave and skillful driver, and won his share of glory, although never enough to satisfy Emilio. He couldn't remember a single word of praise, or a look of fatherly love and pride. His loneliness had made him the perfect target for Dawn. He'd married her, thinking that at last he'd found something that would fill the empty place in his heart. She'd soon shown him his mistake.

But with Louisa's birth, the miracle had happened. When he held the tiny baby in his arms, he'd known that at last here was someone who would return his love with an equal unquestioning love.

It seemed to him quite natural to pick up his baby and hold her against him. The tiny starfish hand, laid in his own palm, had been a delight, and the first time she reached out eager fingers to explore his face, he'd felt the sun come out for him. Dawn laughed at his demonstrativeness, but he informed her that he was no cold-blooded man, but an Italian with a father's heart. For in that nation of child worshippers, Emilio had been an aberration.

His child was the only source of love that had never betrayed him. Everyone else—his father, his mother, his wife—had taught him to fear emotion for the pain it could bring.

But last night he'd been swept by feelings that no amount of caution could stifle. He'd laid down with his enemy, and they'd brought each other profound joy. Now he was wracked by confusion. His heart reached out to her, but his head reminded him that they were still opponents. Whatever was growing between them could never come to fruition until she returned his daughter, not only because he wanted Louisa, but because he longed to feel that Serena was on his side. Only then would he be free to love her.

He leaned down and brushed his lips tenderly against her nose. But almost at once he was interrupted by the sound of distant ringing. He realized that it was his own telephone that he'd left on the hall table last night. He hurried out and down the stairs to snatch it up. "Yes?"

"I've found her," came Banyon's voice.

His heart lurched. "Are you sure?"

"Quite sure. She's living in the midlands in a village called Claverdon."

"There's no mistake?"

"She's the image of the second picture you gave me."

"All right." Carlo lowered his voice. "I'll call you back. Do nothing until you hear from me." He hung up quickly.

A storm of conflicting emotions raged in him. Beneath the joy and relief was dismay that this should happen before Serena told him of her own accord. He would be as ruthless as he had to be to get Louisa back, but he didn't want to be ruthless with Serena. He wanted to be close to her.

Returning to the bedroom, he found her still asleep. He sat on the edge of the bed and began to kiss her. She awoke at once, smiling up into his eyes. "Sleepyhead," he murmured.

"I didn't dream it, did I?" she whispered.

"No, you didn't dream it," he told her. "For if you did, then I must have dreamed it, too, and I couldn't bear that." He gathered her into his arms, raining small kisses on her lips, her neck, reminding her silently of the feelings that united them, and praying for skill and tact in what he had to do now.

"Serena," he said softly.

"Mmm?"

"Didn't you feel, last night, that something wonderful had happened between us?" he ventured.

She gave a smile that stirred him to the depths. "You know that I did."

"I mean more than our passion," he urged. "I mean a much greater closeness, without which passion is hollow. Tell me where your heart was last night."

She laughed, a soft, husky sound that almost destroyed his control. "Tell me where you think it was," she teased.

"I dared to hope that it was close to mine. But now—" he hesitated, feeling the ice thin beneath him.

She frowned. "But now?"

"How can I feel close to you when you still act as my enemy? Now that we've found each other—surely you see that the moment has come for you to tell me where to find Louisa—to give her back to me—" He was praying frantically for her understanding.

But almost at once he realized that it had all gone wrong. He felt her stiffen in his arms, and a mask of caution and reserve obliterated the light that had glowed on her face. She looked at him silently for a moment, before trying to push him away. "I see," she said briefly.

"What do you think you see?" he demanded, still holding her, trying not to admit that he'd failed.

She shook herself free and got out of bed, pulling on a robe. "I should have realized that everything was leading up to this," she said bitterly. "Getting Louisa back. That's what it's all been about, hasn't it?"

Her hostility goaded him to retort, "What did you expect? That I was going to forget about my daughter?

She's been on my mind every moment—*almost* every moment—''

"You said it right the first time," she flung at him. "*Every* moment, including last night, when you held me in your arms and I thought—" She gave a shuddering sigh. "Well, never mind that now."

"But I do mind," he said passionately.

Serena gave a hard laugh. "Of course, because it didn't work. But it nearly did. I congratulate you. You actually had me wondering if I'd misjudged you, if there was more to you than an iron fist. It was a good act, but you spoiled it by moving in for the kill too soon."

He was very pale. "Is that really what you believe, that when I held you—when we held *each other*—it was nothing but an act?" She stared at him defiantly. Anger, incredulity and desperation warred with him, and suddenly he seized her, pulling her hard against him and crushing her mouth with his own. "Was this an act?" he said harshly against her lips. "Did it mean nothing?"

His tongue was in her mouth before she could answer, flickering urgently against her soft inner skin, seeking to evoke memories of the passion that had flowered in the night. But it was cold daylight now, and although her body trembled against his, he sensed the freezing rejection in her flesh. The inner voice of caution shouted to him not to go on with this for fear of losing everything. Somehow he forced himself to release her, pulling away so abruptly that she fell onto the bed and lay looking at him with hate. The sight sent a pain like a knife through him, and he turned to slam both fists down on the dresser in despair.

After a frightful silence he said in a muffled voice, "You must think I'm the most monstrously inhuman man that ever lived."

"I think...I think you're a man who'd do anything he had to to get what he wanted," she said in a shaking voice.

"I want my daughter," he shouted. "Is that so wrong?"

"No, I don't blame you. I can't even blame you for your methods. I blame myself. I knew what you were like. Dawn warned me." Her voice took on a note of bitterness that broke his heart despite himself. "I was a fool to forget."

"Serena, I swear to you it isn't like that. What happened between us last night was bound to happen. Don't tell me you didn't feel that yourself."

He saw the inner struggle written on her face and dared to hope. "Serena, please—think," he pleaded. "Remember. Don't spoil what we have."

"It was you who spoiled it," she said bleakly. Suddenly her voice rose to a cry. "Why did it have to be the first thing you said?"

"It wasn't—" he stammered.

"Oh, you dressed it up with a few pretty phrases first, but in effect it was the first thing you said, and you know it. You were fairly blatant."

He could feel his last chance slipping away, and now, when he most needed his fluent tongue, the words jumbled together in his head. "I didn't mean it to be—blatant—it was just—Serena, I can't explain, but you must tell me where Louisa is. You must tell me *now*. Don't ask me to explain, just try to trust me."

At the word "trust" she turned her head and gave him a little smile with a hint of mockery, either for him or herself. But only her lips smiled. Her eyes had a terrible, withdrawn look that made his heart fail him. How could this be the woman who'd lain in his arms last night, welcoming him into her heart and body? She was a stranger. "Give up," she said at last in a freezing tone that she didn't recognize. "It's failed. It was a clever try but it didn't work."

"Is that all you have to say to me?" he asked in despair. "Because if so, it was all a ghastly mistake. You aren't the only one who was a fool to forget. *I* forgot that you're Dawn's cousin. You even look like her when you have that hard expression on your face. I should have known better than to expect generosity or understanding from one of your family."

He turned from her and flung on his clothes. The spell that had held him in thrall was smashed irretrievably, and now he could see it for the paltry, tinsel thing it had really been. He left the room, hurried down the stairs and snatched up his telephone from the hall table. A moment later he was in his car, quickly starting the engine and turning it out of the drive. He couldn't wait to put as much distance as possible between them.

Five

On the way back to London, Serena's thoughts tossed this way and that. The sound of the front door slamming behind Carlo, and his car driving away, had shocked her out of her anger into chill dismay. An insistent little voice began to ask whether it was really so terrible that he should have asked her about Louisa. If last night had been real—and every fiber of her being clamored to believe it had—then wasn't it natural that he should hurry to end the one conflict keeping them apart?

In the next moment she was arguing the other way, castigating herself for falling into Carlo's trap. She kept it up until her mind shut down from weariness. But on the drive home the questions started up again. By the time she reached her apartment, she was ready to believe that she'd judged Carlo too hastily. She needed to see and talk to him again.

But she didn't know the name of his hotel or the number of his telephone. She could do nothing but wait by her own phone until he called. She stayed in the apartment while the day dragged on, running over the terrible words they'd said to each other, trying to drive from her flesh the memory of ecstasy in his arms. Her head ached with the strain, and she began to feel that she would do anything, give anything, if only he would call.

At last the phone rang and she snatched it up in joyful relief. *"Carlo..."*

But it wasn't him. The disappointment was like a blow in the stomach.

"Serena—it's Celia." Serena's free hand clenched. Something tearful and distraught in Celia's voice filled her with foreboding. "Oh dear, I don't know how to tell you this—"

Serena managed to ask, "What's happened?"

"Louisa's gone. I went to fetch her from school, and she wasn't there. Her father came to collect her. I'll never forgive myself—"

Somewhere deep inside, Serena's heart was breaking, but the words she forced out were steady. "But hadn't you told them never to let Louisa go with anyone but you?"

"Of course, but the headmistress said he was such a very determined man, who simply *insisted* on his own way, and he was obviously her father—I mean Louisa recognized him—" Celia broke off with a sob.

Slowly Serena put down the receiver, wondering bitterly how she could have been such a blind fool. Dawn had told her long ago how charming Carlo could be when it suited him, and how quickly the charm vanished when he had no further use for it. She'd thought herself forewarned and forearmed, yet she'd walked blindly into his trap.

A determined man who insisted on his own way. It was a perfect picture of Carlo. Everything he'd said or done since he came to England had been aimed at this one end. *Everything*.

She took a deep breath and pulled herself together. He'd probably had time to get out of the country, but she could check that. She dialed a number, and after a moment found herself speaking to Harry, a retired policeman with excellent contacts, who owed her a favor. He grunted as she explained what she wanted, and promised to call her back.

He called in ten minutes. "They left for Rome on a privately chartered plane half an hour ago," he said. "The little girl was on her father's passport."

She thanked him, hung up, and sat staring into space. *The little girl was on her father's passport.*

He couldn't have managed that without first getting hold of Dawn's passport. And she'd handed him Dawn's personal possessions, thinking perhaps he had a softer side after all. He'd played her for a sucker all down the line, and she'd fallen for it.

Her heart contracted with pain at the memory of last night, and what she'd thought it meant. She wouldn't let herself think of what he'd said to her, but when she remembered the things she'd said to him she blushed for shame. What a good laugh she'd given him!

Then she checked herself, as though she could blot out the anguish by an effort of will. She had no time now to think of her own suffering. The battle wasn't over. It had merely moved into a different phase.

The huge Valetti mansion was on the ancient Appian Way, just outside of Rome. Serena's heart sank as the taxi approached and she saw the wrought iron gates, firmly locked. But when she gave her name to the lodge keeper, he nodded and immediately opened up. So Carlo was expecting her, she thought.

It was late spring, and the airlines were out on strike. Serena had considered the delay that faced her and booked a seat on a train instead. The journey had taken nearly two days and now, as the car glided up the long drive to the house, she didn't feel girded for battle. She felt stiff, tired and in need of a shower.

She gave her name to the housekeeper, who showed her in to a small room overlooking the garden. While she waited, Serena looked about her, taking in the surroundings. The indications of wealth were spread about with a naturalness that was almost casual. The floor was cool, gleaming marble, and the light fittings about her head were made of expensive crystal. The Valetti family bought only the best as a matter of course. After a moment a maid entered with a tray of coffee that she placed on a low table, underlining Serena's conviction that she was expected. She was on Carlo's home ground now, where he had all the advantages. That was the message.

She sipped the coffee, which was made to perfection, and went to stand by the French doors, which stood open, looking out onto an extensive lawn. Suddenly a pony cantered into view, bearing a small figure in riding clothes and hard hat. As Serena watched, pony and rider sailed over a low jump, landing easily. Then the rider looked up and gave a cry of joy as she saw Serena. She jumped down from her mount, tossed the reins to a groom, and hurled herself at Serena.

Serena gasped as she felt the young arms close tightly around her. "Serena, Serena..." the child cried eagerly.

Her joy broke Serena's heart, because it seemed to confirm that Louisa had indeed been brought back against her will. "Darling, I'm sorry," she said fervently. "I thought you were safe, but I was wrong." Louisa answered with a stream of incoherent Italian that Serena tried to calm. "Hush, I don't understand you. But it's wonderful to see you again. If only—"

The movement of Louisa's eyes made her turn sharply to see Carlo standing there, regarding her coldly. "I've been expecting you," he said.

"As well you might," she told him grimly.

"Papa—" Louisa began.

"Not now, *piccina*. You can talk to Serena later. Go and ride your new pony."

Louisa turned obediently and walked away. The other two regarded each other warily. To Serena's sharp eyes, Carlo looked pale and haggard, and not at all like a man who'd just deceived his enemy to pull off a victory. "I said I was expecting you," he observed, "but I'm not sure why you bothered to come. We fought. I won. It's very simple."

"It's not simple at all, because I haven't given up," she flashed.

Carlo's lip curled. "You're in Italy now, and I'm Louisa's father. If you're stupid enough to challenge me, you'll find that my authority is *absolute*."

She looked at him with cold anger. This must have been how he'd talked to Dawn, threatening her with his "absolute authority," tyrannizing her until she'd been driven to infidelity and then to flight. Oh, but he had other weapons too, she knew that now; subtle, cruel weapons that misused passion and tenderness to break a woman's heart. Anger curdled into hatred as she recalled how she'd lain in his arms, half-delirious with joy at the pleasure and sweetness raging through her, how she'd melted at the soft words he'd whispered in her ear. And every one of them had been false.

She forced the memories back lest they should threaten her control, and regarded him cynically. "A new pony," she said. "I seem to recall that last time it was a new doll. Do you really think you can buy her?"

"I don't have to buy my daughter's affection," he told her sharply. "It's already mine."

"Is it?" she demanded incredulously. "Can't you tell the difference between love and fear?"

Before her eyes, Carlo was transformed. She'd seen him angry before, but not possessed by this black, murderous rage. "Don't ever dare to say such a thing again," he ordered her in a voice that was no less alarming for being soft. "Never so much as hint that my child fears me. Never even think it. Do you understand?"

"Perfectly," she said, refusing to heed the leap of apprehension in her heart. "You want me to know that no one need be afraid of you, and to underline the point, you use threats."

His mouth twisted sardonically. "I said that *my daughter* need not fear me. I never mentioned anyone else. Perhaps you should remember that."

"Are you threatening *me?*"

"We're enemies, aren't we? What else do enemies do?"

Against her will she was pervaded by fresh memories of his arms like steel about her, tense in passionate, tender possession, the warmth of his bare skin next to

hers, the heat of his loins, the thrilling scent of his
arousal: enemies.

Meeting his eyes, she saw her thoughts mirrored
there, and for a moment an echo of her own anguish
flickered across his face. She thought he would say
something but at that moment the housekeeper appeared. Carlo took a deep breath, seeming to shake
himself free of a trance, and gave the woman some terse
commands in Italian. When she'd gone he said, "I've
told Valeria to have your luggage taken to your room.
You'll stay here tonight and leave in the morning."

"Will I indeed?"

He turned on her. "Unless you prefer to leave this
instant, *yes*."

She backed away from the argument. Carlo held too
many cards. Her first priority was to stay and talk to
Louisa.

She became aware that they were no longer alone. A
startlingly handsome young man had appeared through
the French doors and strolled onto the lawn, looking
about him with easy assurance. *"Ciao,"* he hailed them
cheerfully.

Carlo's mouth tightened as he regarded the new-
comer. "Good afternoon," he said stiffly.

"Why are were talking English?" the young man en-
quired with an expressive lift of the eyebrows.

Carlo indicated Serena. "Out of courtesy to this lady,
who comes from England, and does not understand
Italian. But I see no need for you and I to talk about
anything."

"How unkind when I've come to pay you a friendly
visit," the young man said plaintively. His eyes swept
over Serena, and a light of sudden interest gleamed in
them. *"Bella signorina*—you understand that, I'm sure.

It means 'beautiful young lady.' I am so happy to meet you. My name is Primo Viareggi.'' He kissed her hand with elaborate courtesy.

His face had struck Serena as familiar, and now she knew why. Primo Viareggi was a brilliant racing driver, strongly tipped to win the World Championship. He was also, it seemed, a professional charmer. She smiled briefly. "My name is Serena Fletcher," she said.

"Ah, then you are related to Dawn? Her name was Fletcher."

"She was my cousin."

"Then I'm even more delighted to meet you. I had the greatest admiration and respect for Signora Valetti and now I look at you, I can see there is a resemblance."

"There's no resemblance," Carlo insisted quickly. "None at all. What are you doing here, Viareggi? How did you get in?"

"I told your gateman you'd summoned me urgently. It may not have been true, but it should have been. We need to talk."

"We have nothing to talk about," Carlo snapped.

"On the contrary. You've damaged my professional reputation," Primo said in a smooth voice through which a hint of steel gleamed. "Your manager was all ready to sign me up as your driver for this season. I'd turned down several lucrative offers to drive for you, and then you went back on the deal at the last moment. I can't take that lying down."

"I didn't go back on anything," Carlo snapped. "There was never any chance of you driving for Valetti."

"Your manager didn't think so."

"Capriati didn't listen to what he was told. I made my position plain, but he thought he could change my mind by presenting me with a fait accompli. He discovered his mistake."

"Perhaps he thought you'd be influenced by the fact that I'm the best," Primo suggested. "Valetti cars *need* the best. In other words, you need me."

Carlo threw him a black look and turned to Serena. "You'll be wanting to go to your room. Valeria will show you the way."

As she climbed the stairs of the mansion, Serena glanced out of a window on a small landing and saw Louisa cantering away on her pony, a groom mounted beside her. It wasn't hard to guess that Carlo had given the groom orders to keep her away from the house.

Valeria led her to a luxurious room on the other side of the house. It had two floor-length windows that looked out over the countryside. In the distance she could hear the tolling of a bell. "Rome is over there," Valeria said, indicating with her arm. "When it's dark you can just see the lights." She lifted the small suitcase onto the bed.

"Thank you, but no," Serena said quickly. "I'd rather do it myself." She wanted to be alone. When Valeria had gone she stood at the window, looking out over Rome, which had been a magical city to her ever since Dawn had announced that she was going to live there. Now it was a place of bitterness.

From below she could hear the sound of men's voices; Primo's raised in anger, Carlo's cold and ironic. She couldn't understand Italian, but the dislike on both sides was plain enough—even, perhaps, something stronger than dislike. She looked over her balcony and saw Primo storm out and get into his car, while Carlo observed him from the step. The next moment Primo roared off.

Now was her chance. She hurried out of the room and made for the stairs, reaching them just as Carlo appeared in the hall below. He stopped when he saw her, and the way he tightened his lips told her he was preparing himself for battle. Serena went down to meet him. "I want to see Louisa," she said firmly.

He was blocking her path. "I won't let you upset her with a scene."

"I'm not going to make a scene, but I want to ask her how you dragged her back here."

He looked at her, his face cold and impassive. "You're a very stupid woman," he said quietly. "When Louisa saw me she ran into my arms, but I dare say you'll find some excuse not to believe that." When he saw her hesitate, he took her arm and said, "If you want to abuse me let's go somewhere more private."

He guided her downstairs and through a set of double doors into a room furnished as a study. All the way down he kept his hand on her arm, the strong fingers communicating memories that evoked treacherous feelings. She wished he wouldn't touch her. It made it too hard to keep her wits about her, and she would need her wits.

"How strange that we should be meeting like this," he said when he'd closed the doors behind them. "I thought we'd said all there was to say."

"In other words, you feel you've won and therefore the subject is closed," she retorted bitterly. "To think I was fool enough to begin to trust you."

"To think *I* was fool enough to expect warmth and understanding from you," he answered. "We were both fools, but we deluded ourselves most of all. We should never have forgotten that we were enemies.''

''How did you find her?''

''By engaging a private detective, of course.''

''Of course.'' She gave a mirthless laugh. ''And in the meantime you'd tricked me out of her passport—''

''Don't expect me to feel guilty about anything I had to do to recover my daughter,'' he said harshly. ''She's where she belongs, and she's staying here.''

''A detective,'' she mused bitterly. ''And after all the trouble you took that morning, trying to get me to tell you where Louisa was. What a pity you wasted the effort.''

''You don't understand,'' he said somberly. ''I already knew.''

She turned disbelieving eyes on him. ''You—*what?*''

''He called me while you were still asleep and said he'd found her.''

''And when you were begging me to tell you—that was a deception, too?'' she asked in stunned outrage.

''I didn't mean it as a deception. Can't you understand? I wanted *you* to tell me. I thought we'd been close, but I needed you to show that you trusted me. That's why I tried to hurry you, because soon I'd have to admit that I knew, but it would be so much better if you told me yourself. Can't you see that?''

''All I can see is that nothing you say or do can be taken at its face value. There's always something else going on behind it. No wonder Dawn wanted to get Louisa away from you. She didn't want her growing up like you, nor do I.''

''That is unfortunate,'' Carlo said cuttingly, ''because Louisa is my daughter, who will grow up in my house, under my rules. That is my decision, and I warn you most seriously against challenging it.''

If only she could tell him the truth, that he was expending his possessiveness on a child who wasn't his. But she had no idea who Louisa's true father might be, and to speak now would be dangerous and futile.

Carlo watched her pacing the room, trying to tell himself that he felt nothing for her, that he was enjoying his triumph. But the sight of her ravaged face spoiled it for him. There were shadows under her eyes as if she hadn't slept. He thought of his own nights since the night they'd spent in each other's arms, the hours he'd lain awake, aching for her, beating back the thought of her; and all for nothing. Whenever he slept, she was there beside him, beneath him, enticing him, driving him wild with the bittersweet memory.

He would awake, cold and trembling, and force himself to remember who she was, and that there could never be peace between them. The faint resemblance to her cousin that came and went would be there in his mind, stiffening his resolve never to trust one of her family again.

But there was no sign of the resemblance now. Serena simply looked battered and unhappy, and he had a sudden overwhelming urge to enfold her in comforting arms. It was so strong that he had to clutch the edge of his desk, fighting to regain control, praying not to weaken. This woman was dangerous to him, and he would never be safe until he'd sent her away.

''You can see Louisa tonight, and tomorrow you leave,'' he said abruptly, and walked out of the room.

Serena had one hope left—that Louisa would plead for her to stay longer. But when they met at supper that evening she saw a change in the child. She smiled but her liveliness of the afternoon had vanished. When Serena said "hello," Louisa whispered, *"buona sera,"* which surprised Serena, because she knew Louisa's English was excellent.

The three of them dined on the terrace. It was a superb meal, well cooked and perfectly served, in beautiful surroundings. The dusky evening was lighted by candles, and in other circumstances Serena would have reveled in her situation. As it was, she'd never known a more uncomfortable meal. Her attempts to converse with Louisa were painful. The child seemed to have forgotten most of her English, struggling to find the simplest words, and Serena had no doubt of the reason. Whatever Carlo might try to pretend, the truth was that in his presence Louisa was struck dumb with nerves. Rage rose within her.

At last Carlo said, "I think it's time for you to go to bed now, *piccina.*"

Louisa looked at him and asked something in Italian, in which Serena could only make out her own name. At once a dark shadow crossed Carlo's face and he shook his head, saying, "No," with a firmness that sounded angry. Louisa slipped down from her chair and came around to Serena, who'd thought of a way to outwit Carlo.

"Why don't I come up with you?" she said, brushing the hair back from Louisa's eyes. "Then we can—" She broke off with a quick gasp.

"What is it?" Carlo demanded quickly.

"I think you should get a doctor," Serena said, her hand on Louisa's burning forehead.

Carlo touched the child's face and swore under his breath. In a moment he was on the phone, snapping out some orders. When he'd finished he picked Louisa up in his arms and strode from the room. Serena followed them upstairs, her heart beating with apprehension.

The lighting on the balcony had been dim. By the better light in Louisa's bedroom they could see how flushed her face was. "How long will that doctor be?" Serena demanded.

"Not long. She doesn't live far," Carlo said tersely.

Dr. Maria Vini arrived in a few minutes. She was a tall, elegant woman in her fifties, with a calm, reassuring manner. She took Louisa's temperature and listened to her chest, although she was slightly hampered by the fact that Louisa wouldn't let go of Serena's hand. "This is my late wife's cousin, who is paying us a brief visit," Carlo explained.

At the word "brief" Serena felt Louisa's hand contract on her own with a convulsive movement. The doctor's face remained impassive, but Serena had a feeling that she'd seen, and understood a great deal.

"Perhaps I could have a word with the two of you," the doctor said quietly.

When the three of them had gone down to Carlo's study, he said raggedly, "For pity's sake, what's the matter with her?"

"I don't think she has any physical illness at all," Dr. Vini said. "She's a tense, unhappy child, who's lost her mother. Some children react to stress in this way. She made it pretty clear what she wants." She looked directly at Serena. "She wants *you*."

Carlo's head jerked up. "She still has a father," he said.

"But it's her mother she's missing," the doctor pointed out. "To her, the *signorina* is a connection with her mother, and she needs her here. That's my prescription.''

"Then I'll stay," Serena said at once. "But are you sure it's not a severe chill?"

"Reasonably sure. I'll return tomorrow, and I think her temperature will be down." She began to get her things together.

"I'll show you out," Carlo said bleakly.

He escorted her out to her car. While he was gone, Serena ran quickly upstairs to Louisa's room. "How would you like me to stay with you for a long visit?" she asked, sitting on the bed.

Louisa's answer was a beaming smile, the first she'd given all evening, and an eager hug. Serena returned it in full measure, giving thanks with all her heart for her reprieve.

She looked up to find Carlo standing in the doorway, watching them, with a look on his face that wasn't anger, but a kind of sadness, and something else that she couldn't read. She rose and followed him down into the study. "Thank you," he said heavily. "It'll be a damned uncomfortable position for both of us, but if she needs you—"

"We don't have to see too much of each other," she said. "Let's be thankful it's nothing worse. It might have been . . ." Without warning, her voice shook, and to her horror she found tears beginning to run down her face.

"Serena . . ." He took a step toward her.

"It's all right," she said hastily, taking out her handkerchief and dabbing her eyes. "It was just—her having a fever. That's how it was with Dawn—her eyes glittering and her face flushed, and for a moment I thought—I was afraid—" She knew the words were coming out jumbled but she couldn't help it. "I thought she'd be all right—just a chill—and she was so strong— then suddenly—" She pulled herself together. "I'm all right now, really I am."

She turned away quickly, so absorbed in the effort to control herself that she didn't see his hand raised to touch her in comfort, or his face, haggard and defenseless at the sight of her grief.

"I'm staying with Louisa tonight," she said when she was herself again. "I'll go up now."

He was about to say that he'd planned to stay with his child himself, but he paused, realizing that he'd only be in the way. Louisa had shown whom she wanted. The sudden pain stopped him in his tracks, and he stood, with his head bowed, while Serena left the room.

Six

As she had said, Serena spent the night in Louisa's room. Several times Carlo looked in and went to lay his hand on the sleeping child's forehead. By morning it was obvious that Dr. Vini had been right. Louisa's temperature fell sharply, and she woke up looking bright and cheerful.

"She needs your help to get over her mother's death," Carlo said when they were alone. "I won't interfere. But what about your business?"

"Julia, my assistant, can run it for a while. I'll call her and make some arrangements."

"Shouldn't you get some sleep first? You look worn out."

"Later. First I'd like my room moved so that I'm next door to Louisa."

The move was made first thing after breakfast. Serena found herself in a room that was much smaller than the guest room, but less intimidating. She opened a closet door to hang up some clothes, then stopped, staring at the profusion of garments that already hung there. Quickly she opened the other closet and found it full of costly designer dresses, coats, slacks, sweaters, scarves and shoes. She took out an evening dress and examined the low-cut bosom and the high slit sides. It was a vulgar creation, designed to titillate every man in sight, indiscriminately. And it was Dawn's size.

"They belonged to the *Signora*," Valeria said, watching her. "There are only four closets in her room, so she used this one as an overflow."

When Valeria had gone, Serena studied the ridiculous profusion of clothes, feeling oddly disturbed. Perhaps Dawn had bought things she didn't need, to cover her unhappiness. But although this argument helped a little, Serena had too much common sense to believe in it totally. Her beloved cousin's image had become a little blurred.

Living under the same roof as Carlo wasn't as hard as she'd feared. Gradually a routine imposed itself. When Louisa had gone to school, Serena would get on the phone to Julia to keep tabs on the business. All this had to be done in the morning, for the Italian school day started at eight and ended at two in the afternoon. Promptly at 1:45, Antonio, Carlo's chauffeur, started the car to go and wait at the school. Serena decided to go, too, and had her reward in the eager smile on Louisa's face when she saw her.

The two of them usually had the evening meal with Carlo, and Serena was forced to realize that their relationship was warmer than she'd believed. Louisa's silence of the first evening had obviously been due to her temperature, and now she chatted easily to him. The first day Serena came to meet her, she told him all about it. "If you like, I'll come every day," Serena offered. Louisa nodded, and Serena added, "It'll be almost like when your mother collected you."

At once she cursed herself for her clumsiness, for Louisa's smile faded instantly, and soon afterward she asked permission to leave the table. "I'm sorry," Serena said when they were alone. "It was stupid of me to remind her of Dawn."

"That wasn't why she was upset," Carlo informed her. "You made her remember that her mother never bothered to collect her."

"I don't believe that."

He shrugged. "Ask Louisa. I imagine you'll believe *her*."

"I'm not going to upset her by raising the subject again," Serena said firmly.

After lunch she and Louisa would spend the afternoon together, usually riding, which was Louisa's passion. At eight years old she was already a skilled and brave horsewoman, who would never be content until she'd ridden Restif, Carlo's horse, and the most dangerous animal in the stable. He prohibited her firmly from even going near the beast, and the little girl listened in apparently meek silence. But Serena saw the rebellious gleam in her eye.

"There won't be any more trouble now," he told Serena as he left the house one morning.

"I wish I was as sure. I can't keep up with her on a horse, and she knows it." Her own childhood mount had been a placid old pony, and Carlo's thoroughbreds had her at a disadvantage.

"Look, you heard what I said to her just now. She knows I mean it, and she won't give you any trouble."

It was clear he regarded his authority as beyond question, but Serena was beginning to realize that Louisa didn't share that view.

She was proved right with alarming speed. That same afternoon Louisa suddenly spurred her pony into action and galloped away, leaving Serena behind. By the time Serena reached the stables, Louisa had managed to mount Restif and was putting him at a jump. Serena cried out in protest, but her voice was drowned by another cry. Carlo, returning early, was in time to see Louisa soar over the jump, land raggedly and lose her seat. The next moment they were both running across the grass to where she lay.

Serena uttered a prayer of thanks as she saw the child get to her feet. Carlo reached her first, blurting out a sharp question in Italian. Louisa shook her head.

"Thank God she's not hurt," Serena said. "That's all that matters."

But Carlo's temper exploded. His face was a deathly color, and there was a terrible note in his voice. He was speaking rapid Italian, but Serena didn't need to understand the words to know that he was murderously angry. The child listened to him with a pale, set face, then turned and fled. "Did you have to do that?" Serena demanded furiously.

"Yes," he snapped. "I had to. I *had* to because I don't want my daughter to end up with a broken neck."

"All right, so you're upset, but she's bruised and knocked about. You could have told her off later."

Carlo turned on her, his eyes blazing in his ashen face. "Stay out of things you don't understand."

"I understand a hurt, frightened little girl." She turned away but was stopped by Carlo's hand gripping her wrist. "Let go of me at once," she demanded, outraged.

"I want to know where you're going."

"To comfort Louisa."

"Stay away from her. I can say anything that needs saying."

"You?" she echoed scathingly.

He was still holding her wrist. He was calmer now, but his eyes glinted with a light that seemed full of menace. "You think you know everything," he said. "But you know nothing—nothing at all. I warn you, don't try to interfere between me and my daughter again."

He strode away, leaving Serena glaring after him. She went slowly into the house, thinking with pity of the child exposed to so much terrifying rage, with no one there to protect her. Suddenly her resolve stiffened and she hurried upstairs to Louisa's room, running the last few steps to throw open the door.

But on the threshold she stopped, riveted by a completely unexpected sight. Louisa was sitting on Carlo's lap, leaning against him, an arm contentedly about his neck. He was holding her in a protective embrace, one hand stroking her hair, while he whispered gently, *"Perdona me, piccina... perdona me..."*

He looked up at Serena's entrance and for a moment his eyes met hers over the little girl's head. Serena let out her breath and began to back away until she could close the door quietly.

Halfway down the stairs she met Valeria. "I want you to tell me something," she said. "What does *perdona me* mean?"

"It means 'forgive me,'" Valeria explained.

"Thank you. I only—that is, I was just curious."
Serena hurried away from Valeria's puzzled expression.

That evening Louisa came down to supper with her
hand tucked in Carlo's and a smile on her face. Carlo
threw Serena a mocking look, but said nothing. Later,
when Serena took her up to bed, she said, "Louisa, is
everything all right?"

"*Si*." The child looked puzzled. "Why?"

"Your father didn't smack you?"

Louisa shook her head. "It was only Mama who
smacked me," she said. "Papa never." She giggled
suddenly. "But he says he will wring my neck if I scare
him again."

It was clear she'd put the whole incident behind her.
Serena kissed her good-night and went downstairs,
thoughtful. Carlo was still in the dining room, and he
poured her a liqueur as she came in. "Are you satisfied?" he demanded.

"Of course. I'm sorry I burst in on you like that."

"I'm glad you did. Perhaps now you'll realize things
aren't as simple as you thought. I lost my temper because I had the fright of my life. Louisa understood,
and she forgave me."

Serena nodded. It was obviously true. "She seems to
have forgotten the whole thing so easily," she said.

"She's like that. Five minutes ago doesn't exist, nor
does tomorrow. All that matters is what she wants to do
now, this minute. It terrifies me because it makes her so
reckless."

"Perhaps she's seen you being reckless."

"Me? I've never been crazy like Louisa can be."

"You've been a racing driver, haven't you?"

"And you think that means taking stupid risks. It doesn't. It means knowing how to take *intelligent* risks. Some racing drivers are reckless, most aren't. The ones that are don't live very long." He groaned suddenly. "Heaven help me, she's talking about being a driver herself when she grows up. I'm doing everything I can to discourage it."

"How?"

"By letting her see all she wants of the racing world now, hoping she'll get bored. To try to keep her out would be to give racing the lure of the forbidden."

In the days that followed, Serena discovered that Carlo was right about Louisa's enthusiasm for motor racing. The first race of the grand prix season was about to take place in Brazil, and the little girl happily lapped up the atmosphere of excitement and questioned her father eagerly. It wasn't lost on Serena that he answered all her questions with no sign of impatience.

On the day of the race, Louisa, Carlo and Serena watched on television together, with Carlo in constant telephone contact with Brazil. Valetti had two cars entered, but they had to settle for second and fourth. The winner, by a clear margin, was Primo Viareggi, driving for the Bedser-Myeer team, who'd snapped him up.

Carlo's manager, who was watching with them, sighed. "He should have been driving for us. Why you had to make a gift of him to our competitors—"

"That will do," Carlo said harshly.

The team returned from Brazil and was immediately plunged into preparations for the next race in northern Italy. "And we'll be going, won't we, Papa?" Louisa asked anxiously.

"Do I have any choice?" he asked, grinning.

So far Serena had seen nothing of Rome. Her chance came when Louisa announced one day that she'd been invited to a party at a friend's house after school, giving Serena a free afternoon as well as morning. This provoked a conflict with Carlo, who wanted her to let Antonio take her into the city. When Serena said she preferred to hire a car and drive herself, Carlo observed dryly, "You propose to drive an unfamiliar car in the Roman traffic? Are you mad? I'm tempted to let you try. You would certainly never be seen alive again."

"In that case," she said firmly, "I'll call a taxi."

"You won't accept this one little favor from me?" he demanded with a touch of savagery. "Can't we call a truce and be civilized?"

"I distrust your truce, and I've already had a taste of Italian civilization. It has its roots in Machiavelli, the man who invented the art of deception. I'll call a taxi."

"Look," he said, but before he could continue, the phone rang and he snatched it up.

Serena just caught the sound of a woman's voice saying, *"Ciao, caro,"* and instantly his annoyed expression changed, to be replaced by a smile. She slipped away to find Valeria, who used the kitchen phone to call a cab firm and hire a car for the whole day.

Wild horses wouldn't have made Serena admit it, but as soon as she was in Rome she understood what Carlo had meant about the traffic. Her driver took shortcuts that involved tearing madly down narrow streets to certain disaster, except that somehow disaster never came. Then they were out into the main streets again, haring down the Via Della Conciliazione to Saint Peter's, which loomed up, larger and more beautiful than she'd ever dreamed, against the impossibly blue sky.

"Is it always like this?" she asked the driver, clinging on as he missed another car by inches.

Guiseppe flashed her a grin over his shoulder, which
she wished he wouldn't do while driving. "I'm afraid
not, *signorina,*" he said. "It's not often we get a day as
good as this."

Serena chuckled. She was beginning to enjoy herself.
She took the shortest tour around the Vatican, promising herself that soon she'd come back to do the full
five-hour tour. By now she was longing for a rest and a
meal, so she gave Guiseppe an hour off and sat down at
one of the outside tables of a restaurant. It was a
charming place, with individual booths made up of
leafy screens, so that she could enjoy the fresh air and
relative privacy at the same time.

The price list gave her a nasty turn, but she decided
to stay anyway, and was rewarded with some of the
most superbly cooked and prepared food she had ever
tasted. By the time she reached the coffee she was in a
mellow mood. As she was draining the cup, she happened to look through the leaves that separated her
booth from the next one. To her surprise she saw Carlo
sitting there, glancing at the menu. She was just wondering whether to speak to him when two people approached his booth and he looked up at them with a
welcoming smile.

Serena watched, unable to tear her eyes away as Carlo
rose and greeted a very beautiful woman with a kiss.
Then he turned to the woman's companion, a young
boy, about twelve years old. Serena stiffened, and her
heart began to beat uncomfortably as she got a better
look at him. He was the image of Carlo, with dark hair,
brilliant eyes and a wide, beautifully shaped mouth.
The two of them seemed delighted at their meeting and

hugged each other with complete absence of embarrassment.

The woman had a deep, throbbing voice full of mystery and laughter. The glimpse Serena had caught of her had revealed that she was several years older than Carlo, but well preserved and still lovely, and her gorgeous voice completed the effect. They were speaking Italian, addressing each other as *caro* and *cara,* which Serena knew by now was a term of endearment.

She must get out of here without being seen, she thought frantically. She paid her bill and contrived to slip silently from the booth. Guiseppe was waiting for her and she got thankfully into the back of the cab. "Where I take you now?" he demanded.

"Anywhere," she said absently.

"Then we go to the Colosseum, where the Christians were thrown to the lions."

She wandered among the ruins of the arena, not listening to the guide or hearing what he said. Her head was thrumming with what she had discovered. That boy was Carlo's son. The resemblance was too dramatic for there to be any doubt. He must have been born when Carlo was little more than a boy himself, and before his marriage to Dawn. And the woman was the boy's mother. She was older than Carlo, and had probably been his first love. When she'd called him this morning, he'd dropped everything to meet her.

A huge traffic jam caused her to arrive home late, and Valeria told her that Carlo had gone to collect Louisa from the party. She watched them come in a little later, smiling at each other. Louisa's happiness in his company struck Serena like a blow. One day Carlo would have to know that she wasn't his. And what would this arrogant, possessive man, with a ready-made

son, do then? Whatever the outcome, it must surely be
heartbreak for Louisa.

Valeria knocked at Serena's door. "*Signorina,* there
is a gentleman on the telephone for you. I have switched
it through."

Serena picked up her bedside extension and heard a
young, accented voice saying, "I am Primo Viareggi.
I've promised myself the pleasure of renewing your ac-
quaintance."

She was instantly alert. This man had been a friend
of Dawn's. "I'm very glad you did," she said.

"Glad enough to have dinner with me tonight?"

"I'll enjoy that."

"Wait for me just outside the gates. I can't collect you
from the door because Carlo won't let me on his property. I'll be there at eight."

At a quarter to eight she was descending the stairs el-
egantly attired in a short evening dress of olive green,
with an embroidered jacket, when Carlo came into the
hall. "I'm having a night out," she informed him.

He frowned. "What about Louisa?"

"She's asleep, and anyway, she knows I'm going out,
and she's all right. I said I'd look after her, not immure
myself in a nunnery."

"Of course you want to enjoy yourself. I should have
thought of that. I can take you out myself tomorrow."

She regarded him cynically. "What an efficient busi-
nessman you are, Carlo. Everything taken care of. But
there's no need for you to trouble yourself. I prefer to
arrange my own dates."

"I think you enjoy misunderstanding me," he said,
exasperated. "I only—you're not going into Rome
alone, surely?"

"I don't think my plans are any concern of yours."

"It's just that I didn't think you knew anyone—" He stopped and his eyes began to glint. "Serena, I'm telling you—don't go out with Primo Viareggi."

"I hope that isn't an order, Carlo, because giving me orders would be a *big* mistake."

"It's a warning. Don't have anything to do with that man. Is it him?"

She took a deep breath. "Good night, Carlo." She took a step forward but he put out a hand to detain her. Their eyes met, both angry. Serena tried to pull away but he still held her, his hand warm on the bare skin of her arm. His touch was affecting her, sending tremors through her, reminding her of another time, when she'd melted in his arms, yielding herself up to the thrilling sensations that led to other sensations and finally to fulfillment—or what she had thought at the time was fulfillment. Did he think she was so easily fooled a second time?

"Let go of me at once," she said with biting emphasis. "And don't ever do this again."

Whatever he saw in her eyes seemed to startle him, because his hand fell away and he moved back to let her pass.

Primo was waiting for her just outside the gate. In his dinner jacket and black bow tie he looked unbelievably handsome and dashing. In another moment they were on the road.

It was dusk as they entered the city, and the showplaces were already floodlit. Coming off the Via Appia Antica they swung left past the ruins of the old Caracalla Baths. "That's where the ancient Romans relaxed in the intervals of conquering new worlds," Primo explained. "The trouble is, some of them still think they rule the world."

"Meaning Carlo?"

"Definitely. To a Roman, only Romans matter. The rest of Italy exists to provide them with inferiors."

"Where do you come from?" she asked, amused.

"Naples, where we're less stiff-necked and know how to enjoy ourselves."

"Where are we going?"

"The Via Veneto. It's a very exciting place. Sadly, the great days are over, but occasionally someone brings them back to life. Dawn could do that. Her personality was pure champagne, and when she was out on the town, *la dolce vita* lived again."

As soon as he drew to a halt in the Via Veneto, flashbulbs began to explode all around them. "One thing hasn't changed," he observed, "and that's the paparazzi."

She followed his lead through a doorway and down some steps, then looked about her, amazed. The modest exterior hadn't led her to expect this sumptuous underground room. A waiter bowed and led them to a reserved table. Clearly Primo was a hero to his countrymen and women. Heads turned as they passed; male eyes regarded them with admiration, female ones with envy. Primo was charming to everybody, acknowledging the cheers, shaking a hand here and there, occasionally bestowing a peck on a woman. At last he sat down at the table with Serena. "Forgive me," he said with a self-deprecating laugh, "I have to do my duty." But she had a feeling that he thoroughly enjoyed the adulation.

"I'm flattered to be with the hero of the hour," she said, toasting him in champagne. "Your win in Brazil was marvelous."

"Thank you." He grinned. "Tell me, was Carlo *very* angry."

"He was angry when someone said you should have been driving for us."

"I should like to have seen that."

"Why won't Carlo let you drive for him?" Serena asked curiously.

"He hates me, for many reasons. We started our careers at the same time, but I was the better driver, and he knew it. His father signed me up for the firm, and for a while we both drove for Valetti. I won more races, and he never forgave me for that.

"Then the old man died, and Carlo left racing to take over the firm. And I can tell you, he was glad to get out. It saved him from having to confront his own failure. I was World Champion twice while I was driving for Valetti. Carlo would never have been World Champion."

"You can't be sure of that."

"But I can. I've driven against him, and I know that he lacks the final ounce of courage that tips the balance. Do you know where races are won? On the corners, because that's where you get the chance to overtake. And when two drivers are going neck and neck into the bend, it's a duel of nerves to see which one of them will brake first. Whoever holds out longest will come out of the bend in front."

"Are you saying Carlo didn't hold out?" Serena asked.

"Not against *me* he didn't," Primo said significantly. "That was another ember on the fire of his hate.

And also—'' Primo hesitated ''—he knew that I was in love with his wife.''

''I wondered,'' she said.

''She deserved happiness, but Carlo wasn't the man who could give it to her. He'd married her as a kind of status symbol, because she was so beautiful. But then he treated her like a piece of property, to be taken up when it suited him, and neglected when he had 'more important' matters to attend to.''

She nodded. ''Yes, I can imagine that.''

''Dawn was a woman of great spirit. She wouldn't put up with his cavalier behavior. We began a flirtation, and before we knew it we were really in love. Carlo found out and forced her to stay away from me. He's a vengeful man, and a possessive one. What's his, is *his*— even if he no longer really wants it. Dawn belonged to him, and anyone who dared look at her was made to suffer.''

''What did he do?''

''Dismissed me the moment he was in charge of the firm, and told me I'd never drive for him again. He spread stories about me, saying I was reckless and unreliable. Some believed it, others just looked at my record. I got a job with another team, but their cars weren't so good, and I crashed. I nearly died, and it was two years before I raced again. I fought back, driving to my limit with inferior cars. Last year I came second in the World Championship. It's not enough. I have to win it again.''

Serena was longing to ask him about Louisa, but finding a way was going to be tricky, especially in this flashy place. She felt that a man with more sensitivity wouldn't have come here, and she couldn't help being a little disappointed in Primo. But she refused to give up. If he was the man Dawn had loved, then there *must* be more to him than met the eye. "Why did you bring me here?" she asked as they were finishing their coffee.

"Because it was Dawn's favorite place," he responded at once. "Come, let me show you where we had fun." He took her hand, pulling her to her feet and drawing her after him across the restaurant to a heavily curtained door. A waiter opened it and they passed through. Serena saw tables covered with numbers, headed by croupiers and surrounded by anxious-faced people. She was in a casino.

Primo led her to a table and they sat down. He gave some orders in Italian, signed a piece of paper and some chips appeared in front of her as if by magic. "No," she protested, trying to push them away. "I don't want—"

"Nonsense. I've already paid for them," he said, pushing them back.

His voice had changed. He was no longer the gallant cavalier, but a man silencing an awkward woman so that he could get on with the main business. Serena gave up the argument and played halfheartedly. To her relief, she won nothing and saw the pile diminish.

But at once another pile appeared in front of her. "Take them," Primo insisted, forestalling her. He spoke without taking his eyes from the table. "You're my lucky mascot. *She* always was."

But his luck was out. He lost, lost again, won a little, then lost everything. He shrugged and signed a paper with a flourish, but Serena caught a glimpse of the amount, and paled. "That must be twenty thousand pounds," she whispered, frantically converting the lire.

"So what? I won a race last week. Next week I'll win another one."

"Primo, I'm not Dawn. I'm not lucky for you."

Abruptly he seemed to lose interest in gambling. "Okay. Let's dance."

He led her into the next room where couples were dancing, and immediately pulled her close. "Does it offend you that I look at you and think of Dawn?" he asked.

"Not at all. I loved Dawn. I want to talk about her."

"You're like her, and yet not like her. She'd never have worried about how much I was losing. She understood the thrill of that moment when one split second can bring you disaster or triumph. It's like racing. At two hundred miles an hour you can be a hero or a dead man, and you never know which it's going to be. It's the most glorious feeling in the world. She knew that. Her philosophy was 'do as you damn well please.' She was a wonderful woman."

"Always doing as you please doesn't sound very wonderful to me," Serena mused. "What about other people?"

"To hell with other people!" he said lightly. "That was another of her philosophies."

"I don't believe she ever said anything of the kind," Serena said with a touch of desperation.

He shrugged. "Have it your way."

There was a little ache in her heart. But he must be exaggerating. Dawn had been reckless and fun-loving, yes. But not the selfish hedonist he was painting.

She became aware that Primo was holding her very closely, in a practiced exaggeration of romance. She tried to draw back but he wouldn't release her. "You're overdoing it," she muttered.

"How can one overdo *l'amore?*" he said huskily.
"Don't you feel your heart beat to the rhythm of
mine?"

"All I feel is my feet beginning to hurt," she said
prosaically. "And I'd like to sit down. There's something I must ask you, Primo—something very important."

"Oh-ho, that sounds intriguing. Very well, let us sit
down, and then—" he looked down intensely into her
eyes "—you can tell me what is in your heart."

Serena sighed, realizing that this was going to be very
difficult. But somehow she had to find out if he could
possibly be Louisa's father, and she might not get the
chance again. So she gave him an artificial smile, and
to her dismay he held her more tightly, nuzzling her
neck.

And then, over Primo's shoulder, she saw Carlo
watching them, his face cold with contempt.

Seven

Carlo paused outside Louisa's bedroom door before turning the handle very softly and looking inside. The room was in near darkness, and he could hear the soft sound of her breathing. He moved quietly across to the bed and stood looking down at her in the dim light that came from a crack in the curtains. He felt like a miser who'd recovered his stolen treasure, and he supposed a miser was what he was. He hoarded her in his heart. He had more worldly goods that he knew what to do with, but she was more to him than all these. Only one other threatened her preeminence, and that love was as hopeless as it had ever been, making Louisa more precious still.

She stirred and opened her eyes, smiling when she saw him. "Papa?"

"Yes, little one?"

"Has Serena come back yet?" she murmured.

His eyes clouded with faint disappointment that her first thought had been for someone other than himself. "Not yet."

"Is it very late?"

"It's one o'clock in the morning."

"Why doesn't she come home?"

"I—suppose she's enjoying herself."

"Without us?"

She spoke innocently, but every word seemed to turn a knife in him. "Serena has—other friends," he said. "We must let her see them sometimes."

"But she belongs to us, doesn't she?" Louisa asked with a sudden urgency in her voice that tore at his heart.

"No, my darling," he said gently. "She doesn't belong to us. She—" He stopped, undecided, then a sudden resolve came to him. "Shall I fetch her for you?"

"Please."

He kissed her and left the room. A few minutes later he was in his car and on the road to Rome. He headed for the Via Veneto without any hesitation, and drew up outside the casino. He was displeased to notice that one lone paparazzo was still on duty, no doubt remembering the old days when Carlo Valetti had come here in search of his wife. The photographer stepped forward, his camera at the ready. "If you want that thing rammed down your throat, just take one picture," Carlo told him with soft menace, and the man backed off at once.

Memories assailed him as he went in. Once Dawn had haunted this place in increasingly dubious company. Now he felt another fear, one he hadn't dared name yet. He spoke briefly with the head waiter, a note changed hands, and a table was pointed out to him. But there was no one there. He drew another blank in the gaming hall and hurried on to the dance floor, his heart filled with foreboding. He knew he risked looking foolish, a man come in search of a woman who'd chosen another man, but he was driven by demons.

At last he saw them and halted on the edge of the dance floor, with his eyes narrowed. They were dancing closely together, Serena held against Primo's body while his lips nuzzled her neck. Carlo froze, trying to brace himself against the pain that assailed him. At that moment Serena saw him and stiffened. As they held each other's eyes he was sure he could read the expression in hers; hostility and defiance, anger that he had come seeking her, coldness at his presumption, but not the understanding he longed for. When he knew he had himself under control, he pushed through the crowd.

"Ah, my friend," Primo greeted him. "Have you come to have a good time?"

Carlo ignored him. "I want you to come home with me," he said to Serena.

Before Serena could answer, Primo swiveled adroitly so that her back was to Carlo, and began to whirl her away across the floor. But she stopped him and disengaged herself, walking away from both of them, back to the table. When Carlo reached her she was sitting down. "I asked you to come home," he repeated.

"I heard you, but I'm not ready to leave," she said frostily. "And just what right do you think you have—"

He wanted to plead with her, to speak of Louisa, and in that softened mood they might reach an understanding, but Primo appeared, settling down beside Serena, and he was struck dumb before his enemy. "Join us," Primo offered, his eyes glinting with malice.

"Is that necessary?" Serena asked quickly.

"The poor fellow's come all this way," Primo pointed out. "We should at least offer him a drink."

Carlo sat down and regarded them. He didn't want this three-way conversation, but he wasn't leaving without her. He waved aside the whiskey Primo pressed on him. "Mineral water," he told the waiter.

"Mineral water," Primo echoed in disgust.

"When I'm driving, yes," Carlo said firmly.

"Naturally," Primo agreed. "One must be cautious at all times." He gave Serena a glance full of malicious conspiracy. "What did I tell you?"

Carlo looked at him with hate. So they'd been talking about him. Primo had poured his poison into her ear, and she'd laughed with pleasure to hear him denigrated. But he controlled himself and said calmly, "There's a time to be cautious and a time for abandoning caution."

"And the time for being cautious is when the race hots up," Primo said significantly, "because otherwise one might get killed—"

"Or kill someone else," Carlo said bitingly.

Primo laughed silently. "You're so clever at excuses," he jeered. "And so virtuous. Ye gods, what a bore!"

"Primo, please," Serena said in a low voice, "this isn't the time..."

"It's the only chance I'll get," Primo snapped. "You don't think he seeks my company for pleasure, do you? Oh no, he avoids me now as he used to do on the track, because of what we both know—"

The last word was choked off as Carlo seized him by the throat. There was a little flurry, and a waiter intervened. Carlo released Primo at once. His momentary lack of control was over, and although his face was gray, he was in command of himself. He pressed a large tip into the waiter's hand and waved him away.

Primo gave a jeering grin. "How useful money can be! Without it you get thrown out of this place for starting a fight. But with it—oh, money has such power. It can buy the best cars, and it can be used to destroy a rival who looks too good." He saluted Carlo mockingly. "How lucky for you, my friend, that you inherited a fortune and were able to leave racing before you were really tested."

Carlo met Primo's eyes across the table, and his own were deadly. "One day," he said softly, "I will make you eat those words in dust." He stood up, taking Serena's arm and forcing her to stand too. "We're leaving," he said.

"The hell you are!" Primo exclaimed. "When I take a woman out, *I* take her home."

"Leave it," Serena told him quickly. "No more fighting."

Carlo's hand tightened. "Come along," he said.

"Are you going to let him tell you what to do?" Primo demanded excitedly. "Dawn never put up with that. She did exactly what she wanted. She had spirit."

"Well, I'm not Dawn," Serena said hastily. "Good night, Primo. Thank you for a lovely evening."

She freed herself and strode out ahead of Carlo. He caught up with her in the darkened street. "The car's this way." He saw her settled and got into the driver's seat. "I'm glad you saw sense," he said as he started up.

"I came with you because I didn't want a scene, that's all. What the hell do you think you're doing?"

"Louisa was asking for you."

"But she knew I was going out. She didn't mind."

"She woke up and was very upset that you hadn't returned." Carlo was conscious of exaggerating a little, but anything was better than letting her suspect the wild jealousy that had driven him in search of her, or the gut-wrenching agony of seeing her locked in Primo's arms, letting him nuzzle her neck.

He remembered how her neck felt, soft and silky under his lips, how cool and elegant it was to kiss, and how a little pulse throbbed at the base of her throat when she became excited . . .

"Careful," Serena cried.

Carlo cursed and wrenched at the wheel, bringing the car out of its swerve. For the rest of the journey he concentrated on the road.

Louisa was hanging over the banister when they reached home, and Serena immediately ran upstairs. Carlo watched from below as they hugged each other, and Serena scooped up the child and carried her, laughing, back to bed. He turned away sharply, because the sight brought him pain that had nothing to do with his wounded sexual pride.

He seldom drank, but now he went straight to the liquor cabinet in his study and poured himself a stiff brandy. He was a fool for minding so much, and he knew it. He'd been to that place before in search of Dawn, but it had never hurt as much as this.

After half an hour Serena returned. She was still wearing the olive green dress, and he noticed how the soft material clung to her. It was the garment of a hypocrite, he told himself bitterly. It seemed so demure, with its high neck and long sleeves, but it emphasized every line of her body, every swell and hollow, every movement. The sight made him ache with longing for what he couldn't have, and he tossed back his drink.

"I want to make it clear," Serena said coldly, "that this is never to happen again. You had no right to haul me out of there as if you were my—my father. I do as I please and I see whomever I please."

"You can do better than that cheap playboy," he jeered.

"That's my business. It doesn't concern you."

"It does if you bring him to this house. Even the gate is too near."

"All right," she snapped. "Next time I'll hire a taxi and meet him in Rome."

"So there's going to be a next time?" he demanded cynically. "Don't be a fool, Serena. Can't you see he's using you to get at me?"

"You flatter yourself."

"Indeed? Do I take it then that this is the start of a great love affair?" He heard the sneer in his own voice and despised himself for it, but he couldn't stop.

"You can take it that you should keep out of my affairs," she snapped.

"Then I wish you well of him. I thought you were a woman of taste."

She turned glittering eyes on him. "Did you? I wonder what can have given you that idea? It couldn't have been the trivial little dalliance we enjoyed in England could it? Because if so, you're not only arrogant and overbearing, you're conceited as well."

He paled. "What are you trying to say?"

"I'm saying that I wanted to discover something— just what Dawn ever saw in you." She gave a short laugh and faced him with chilly eyes. "Frankly it's as much of a mystery to me as it ever was."

He told himself that she didn't mean it; she was only paying him back for his sneering contempt of a mo-

ment ago. But the reassurance was useless against the
pain and misery that assailed him. "You're lying," he
said frantically. "There was something between us that
night, you know there was."

"Only in your imagination."

"And in our bed," he shouted, seizing her. "Don't
lie to me, Serena. There was such heat between us we
nearly burned the place down. You can't fake that kind
of passion."

"You can if you've set your heart on a good laugh,"
she retorted with a curl of the lip that nearly destroyed
him.

If she didn't stop he knew he couldn't be responsible
for his own actions. He wondered wildly if she knew the
risk she was running. The eyes that had shone up into
his at that moment of perfect union were hard and glittering now. The mouth that had offered him such sweet
temptation was smiling dreadfully as the cruel taunts
issued from it. He fixed his gaze on that beautiful
mouth, remembering how the lips had moved, teasing,
inciting, parting...

Suddenly he broke. His hands seemed to tighten on
her shoulders of their own accord, pulling her hard
against him, while he dropped his head until his lips
hovered an inch above hers. "Shut up!" he said with
whispered violence. *"Per l'amor di Dio—silenzio!"*

He crushed her mouth with his own before she could
reply, releasing his pent-up, aching frustration in a
fierce kiss that brooked no refusal. She stiffened in his
arms and he sensed her shock and surprise. He took
advantage of it to deepen the kiss, forcing his tongue
into her mouth with a ruthless insistence that amazed
him. He was a modern man, or so he'd thought. But the
savage emotions that had erupted between them to-

night had stripped away the veneer of modernity, revealing a self he barely recognized, one that was rooted in two thousand years of Roman arrogance and pride of conquest. He came from a race of Caesars, men who had mastered the world, subduing rebellion, and taking, not asking.

He wasn't asking now, but taking something he still thought of as his own, because it had once been offered freely and with such generous fervor that it could never be taken back. Her true gift had been the knowledge of her desire for him. She might want to deny it now, but he knew. He would make her acknowledge it again, and when he'd done so they would rediscover each other in the white heat of passion where tenderness also lived. Then the nightmare of their estrangement would be over.

So he exerted all his skills, seducing, alluring, enticing her, exploring her mouth with the little teasing movements that he knew she loved. He had his reward in the muffled groan that broke from her through the kiss, and in the feel of her breast rising and falling against his as passion claimed her. His hands roved over her body, maddeningly hidden in the clinging dress that suggested but didn't disclose. All hostility was forgotten. He wanted only to claim her, and find with her the love that had somehow eluded them, yet which persistently tantalized him.

His own desire was rising sharply. Want and need fused. Sensation and emotion streamed into each other. His body ached with the craving to possess her, and his heart ached with the loneliness only she could assuage. He heard a voice call her name and realized it was his own. His hand enfolded one breast, teasing the nipple between finger and thumb until he felt it proud and peaked through the material.

"Serena..." he groaned.

Her whispered "yes" thrilled and tortured him. He drew her urgently toward the big leather sofa. In a few moments they would be united again and all sadness would be over. He pressed her back against the cushions, working on the tiny buttons at the front of her dress with trembling fingers. She arched against him as he slipped his hand inside, caressing the silky skin of her breast. He dropped his head to take the nipple between his lips, lost in an erotic joy that seemed to possess his very soul. He wanted to tell her that he loved her, and beg her to love him.

And then he felt her grow still in his arms, and something in that stillness frightened him. He raised his head to look into her eyes, and drew a sharp breath at what he saw there.

Nothing. As cold and bleak a nothing as ever a man had seen in the eyes of a hostile woman. The sight of that nothing made his joy shrivel within him.

"Oh no," she said at last, "not again."

"Serena..."

"Let go of me, Carlo," she said in a warning voice. "Let go now."

Dazed, he did so, breathing hard as he drew away from her. She got up quickly from the sofa and moved away from him, doing up her buttons.

"For pity's sake, Serena, what happened?" he begged

"What happened?" She gave a hard laugh that made him wince. "I learned my lesson, that's what happened. You used me like this once. You won't do it a second time."

If he'd been less distraught he might have remembered her taunt, only a moment ago, that *she* had used *him,* and seen it for the hollow claim it was. But the frustrated clamor of his senses was driving him wild, and he was beyond rational thought. "Used you?" he echoed. "Do you know what you're saying? If words have any meaning for you, how can you call what's between us *using you?*"

"There's nothing between us," she cried raggedly. "Nothing."

"You know better than that. Stop hiding from it and face the truth."

"The only truth I know about you is that you'll stop at nothing," she said wildly. "You take what you want when it suits you and you don't care who you hurt."

"Very well," he grated. "If you're determined to think the worst of me, then think it." Driven half out of his wits he seized her and looked down into her flushed face. "Perhaps you're right. I take what I want, and right this minute, what I want is you."

He smothered her mouth before she could reply. Nothing mattered now but their battle, and that he should emerge the victor. Deep inside him some instinct warned him that she could make him her slave, and his pride demanded that he defeat her before that happened. As long as she could resist their passion, she was stronger than he. So he fought her with every erotic weapon at his command, reminding her with lips and tongue and hands that she belonged to him.

For one brief, glorious moment he thought he'd won. He felt her melting in his arms, her body glowing with the heat that blended with his own and that could have only one end. But it was an illusion. From somewhere she found the strength to struggle free and throw him off. Her eyes were blazing and her voice shook, but she had command of herself.

"I might have expected that," she said raggedly. "You couldn't let this end until you'd had your own way. But not with me. Dawn couldn't fight you, but I can. Now I know exactly why she ran away from you. I won't run, for Louisa's sake, but don't ever again try to behave as though you own me. Be content with the things you do own, Carlo. You'll never have me."

She backed away from him, then turned and ran from the room as though afraid he would follow. But he was suddenly incapable of movement. Her words had struck him like a blow, and all the strength seemed to have drained out of him.

The room was very quiet when she'd gone. Slowly he sat down on the sofa, wondering how he could have ever imagined that this woman was different. The truth was that she was as devious and heartless as the other. She must never know how he'd fallen into her trap. As for the feeling he'd thought was love—it was a sickness and must be fought to the death. If she could be strong, so could he: strong enough to avoid her, and look through her and pretend she didn't exist. And soon he would be cured.

Despairing, he dropped his head into his hands.

For several days Serena didn't see Carlo, and she was glad. The events of that night had left her shattered. The memory of how nearly Carlo had humbled her pride, asserting his dominance in the way she found hardest to resist, sent hot and cold shivers through her whenever she thought of it. She'd been ready to abandon everything for the exquisite joy of making love with him again. But love had no part of what he was doing, and when it was over she would have been forced to face that fact in shame and horror. It was better as it was. At least she'd kept her self-respect.

But then she remembered the last moments, and his stricken look, as though something had died inside him. And her self-respect seemed suddenly tinged with arrogance and cruelty. She hadn't meant to hurt him so badly.

She began to hope for a chance meeting so that she could show him a kinder face, but the chance didn't come. Louisa explained her father's absence by saying he was deep in last-minute preparations for the San Remo Grand Prix. "And he's promised to take me," she said joyously.

One evening he dined at home for the first time in a week and remarked casually, "You'll be glad to see the back of Louisa and me for a few days, I expect. While we're at San Remo, my office in this house is at your disposal."

"Thank you," she said formally, unable to suppress a chill of disappointment in her heart at this plain hint that she wasn't invited. Carlo left the room without speaking again.

A few days later the entire Valetti team, with Carlo and Louisa, set off for northern Italy. Serena watched the race on television, hoping to observe for herself what Primo had meant about overtaking. But he led the race from the moment he streaked off the grid from pole position until he swept across the finishing line under the checkered flag. Only the fact that the other Bedser-Myeer car finished tenth gave her an inkling of his true brilliance. Valetti cars came in second and third.

Louisa arrived home bouncing with excitement and eager to tell Serena every detail. "And Papa has promised to take me to the next race in Monaco," she said. "Oh Serena, it would be so lovely if you could come, too. You will, won't you?"

Before Serena could reply, Carlo interrupted smoothly, "Serena has a lot of work to do. She won't have time to come to Monaco with us."

"That's right," Serena said bleakly. "I'm very busy."

The Monaco Grand Prix, two weeks later, gave her a clearer insight into Primo's skills. Instead of having a special racetrack, the cars drove through the winding streets of the little principality. Valeria, who'd become an expert through ten years of working for the Valetti family, told Serena that overtaking was almost impossible on those tight hairpin bends.

"Whoever gets away first, stays in front," she prophesied.

But they'd reckoned without Primo whose car stalled on the starting line, and who finally got into the race in fifteenth position. For the next two hours they watched him weave, repeatedly challenging other cars with his foot on the accelerator, and always winning the encounter. It was a brave driver who'd take Primo on to the last split second. The two Valetti cars came in first and second, and Primo managing third, a result that still brought him valuable World Championship points.

Valeria snorted with contempt. "He's crazy," she said. "One day he'll kill himself. Trouble is, he'll take someone else, too."

Serena nodded. The race had left her thoughtful. While admiring Primo's ability, she was chilled by the blind self-absorption that led him to bully other drivers to the edge of an accident in his desire for glory.

She returned to the study to send a fax to her office on Carlo's machine. While she was waiting for a page to go through, she looked at some of the photographs on the shelves. She'd noticed them vaguely before, but for the first time it occurred to her that there was something strange about them. Apart from a couple of Louisa, they all celebrated the triumphs of Emilio Valetti.

Valeria entered with a tray bearing coffee. "This room is like a shrine," Serena observed.

"*Si, signorina*. The late master was a vain man. He collected every word that was ever written about himself. You see these books?" Valeria deposited the tray and pulled down a large scrapbook from a shelf. "They are filled with press cuttings in many languages. He had agencies working all over the world to collect everything."

"But what about Carlo? Didn't he ever win races?"

"He won several, but he isn't a man who collects mementos about himself."

"But surely his father..."

Valeria shook her head. "Emilio Valetti collected only the records of his own achievements," she said significantly.

"How terrible!" Serena said, shocked.

Valeria nodded, and departed. Serena began to turn the pages of the scrapbook, wondering what life must have been like with a father so absorbed in himself that he had no time to be proud of his son.

She exclaimed as a loose photograph slipped from between the pages and fell to the floor, and dropped to retrieve it. Then she froze, her heart beating.

It was a picture of the beautiful woman she'd seen at the restaurant, and she was sitting with her arm about the boy who looked so like Carlo.

Eight

Carlo and Louisa reached home the following evening. Louisa flung herself into Serena's arms, bubbling over with details about the race. "I saw it all," Serena told her, smiling.

"You see, Papa, I *knew* Serena was interested," Louisa declared triumphantly. "Papa said you didn't care about racing, but I was sure you did. In two weeks there'll be another race—in Mexico," she finished, with a significant look at her father.

"Neither of us is going to Mexico, *piccina*," he informed her hastily.

"Oh Papa..."

"Racing cars won't pay for those dancing lessons you want," he said, tweaking her hair. "It's the commercial vehicles that do that, and it's about time I gave them some more attention."

"Your new model is due out soon, isn't it?" Serena asked politely.

He seemed to become aware of her for the first time. "Yes," he said shortly.

"Oh, Serena, it's so beautiful," Louisa bubbled. "And Papa says I can come and watch the final trials. You'll come, won't you?"

"Of course I will," she said quickly, before Carlo could close off this avenue, too. "I've been longing to see the new Valetti."

She knew that the firm had taken over a huge stretch of land five miles outside Rome and turned it into a track on which cars could be tested. The trials were set for two days later. At breakfast that morning Carlo spoke briefly to Serena. "I'll take Louisa to the track myself. Antonio will bring you later."

Such a blatant snub took her breath away, and she was on the verge of telling him that she'd skip the trials altogether. But that would hurt Louisa, so she merely nodded.

She occupied herself for an hour after they left and was just tidying up when the phone rang. It was Primo. "Spend the day with me," he said.

"I'm afraid I can't. But I have time for a coffee." She still had something to ask Primo.

"I'll collect you outside the gates in twenty minutes."

He took her to a small roadside trattoria. "It's good to see you again," he said charmingly. "I was worried when he dragged you off that night."

"But not worried enough to call and ask me how I was," she pointed out with a faint smile.

He shrugged. "Well, I wasn't *too* worried. When a man's that crazy about a woman, she can do as she likes with him."

"You've got it wrong," she said wryly. "Carlo is far from crazy about me."

He gave a cynical laugh. "Don't tell me. I'm a man. I can tell when another man is burning up about a woman. He was ready to commit murder."

Serena was silent, staring into her coffee cup, torn by opposing feelings. Her mind was still suspicious of Carlo, but her heart had a wayward independence of its own, and it refused to fall into line. It had given a leap of joy at Primo's assertion that Carlo was crazy about her, and while she uttered the mechanical denial, she'd been shaken by the force of her own longing for it to be true. It was absurd, irrational, but it had seized her and it wouldn't let her go.

"You shouldn't have left without me," Primo added casually. "It was a disaster. I went back to the casino and lost more money."

"Primo, did you mean what you said about Dawn going to the casino?"

"Sure I did. She never cared how much she lost."

"I should think Carlo would, though."

Primo shrugged. "She had ways of bringing him to heel. The first time he made a big fuss she just vanished to England, taking the little girl. That brought him running fast enough." He gave a cynical laugh.

A chill went over Serena, and a kind of rage began to burn in her heart at hearing Carlo traduced by this shallow man. "He loves Louisa," she pointed out.

"Does he, hell! She's his property, an extension of himself. He had to recover her."

"You don't like children, do you?" she said, looking at him curiously.

"They're all right, as long as they don't get in my way. My sister has six kids. That's why I never visit her." He grinned. "I looked for you at Monaco. Pity you weren't there. Did you see the race on television?"

"Yes, I saw it. You're lucky to be alive. So are some of the others."

He gave a careless shrug. "That's the luck of the game. You live, you die. And if you die—who cares, as long as it was a good race?"

"But suppose the others don't feel that way?"

"Sure they do, or they wouldn't be there," he said dismissively.

"Why did you call me, Primo?"

"Ah, you've reminded me. I wanted to know what you were going to ask me that night on the dance floor, just before we were interrupted. You do remember, don't you?"

Serena took a deep breath to speak, but stopped before she could utter. This was all wrong. Surely Primo couldn't be the man for love of whom Dawn had betrayed her husband? Handsome, charming and witty on the surface, he was a blank where his inner self should be. There was no way she could ask him if he was Louisa's father. She could only hope and pray that he was not. "I—no, I'm afraid I don't remember," she said. "It was probably something quite trivial. Look, I have to be getting along. I promised to go to the practice track."

"I'll drop you there."

"There's no need," she said hastily. "Just take me back to the house."

He made a grunt that might have been agreement, but once on the road he swung in the opposite direction. Serena groaned at the thought of arriving with the firm's chief rival, but there was no help for it. When they reached the track, closed off behind huge wire gates, a guard came out, frowning. "I was told you were coming with Antonio," he told Serena. "I'll have to call the boss." He retired behind the fence, carefully locking it behind him, and vanished into his cubicle.

A moment later Carlo appeared from one of the many sheds behind the perimeter fence, and began walking toward them. He was wearing the white overalls of a racer, a skintight garb that showed off his broad shoulders and lean muscular figure. Even at a distance Serena could see that his mouth was hard with controlled anger. Primo had stepped out of his car and was standing with her at the gate. *"Bon giorno,"* he hailed Carlo.

Carlo opened the gate and confronted him. "Let me make it quite clear that you're not welcome here," he said curtly. "I suggest you leave at once. And you—" he turned on Serena, "—perhaps you'd prefer to leave with him."

"Well, I wouldn't," she said firmly. "Louisa is expecting me. Are you going to let me in?"

For a moment she almost thought he would refuse. Then he gave a curt nod and stood back for her to pass. Primo seized her hand before she could snatch it away, dropped a kiss on it and jumped back into the car.

Serena passed through the gate, and after a moment Carlo came up beside her. "My office is this way," he said, steering her into one of the huts. She found herself in an austere functional room, whose walls were lined with charts. Carlo shut the door firmly behind them. "How dare you bring that man here!" he said in a low, furious voice.

"Look, I'm sorry. It was a mistake. I asked him to take me back to the house so that Antonio could bring me here."

"And why were you with him in the first place?" he demanded, his eyes kindling.

"I don't think that's any of your business. I've told you it was a mistake, so please leave the subject."

He gave a mirthless laugh. "Strange how that Neapolitan causes women to make these 'mistakes.' Of course, he's neglected you recently, hasn't he? Are you beginning to learn that he cares for nothing and nobody but himself? Couldn't you have more dignity than to run to him the minute he snaps his fingers?"

"Get one thing straight," she told him, eyes flashing. "There is no man, *no man at all,* who can fetch me by snapping his fingers."

"Fine words, but your behavior disproves them. This morning, at breakfast, you had no idea you were going to see him. Then, one word from him and you dropped everything. I called the house and heard how you rushed out to meet him."

"Were you checking up on me?" she demanded, incensed.

Carlo paled and turned away from her lest his face betray too much. She mustn't suspect that the yearning to have a few minutes alone with her had finally become overwhelming, and against his better judgement he'd really called to say he would return for her himself. He ground his nails into his palm as he remembered the exciting beating of his heart as he dialed the number, and then the dreadful moment when he learned that she'd driven off with his enemy. He could have laughed to think what a fool he'd been, but it would have been bitter laughter.

"Were you checking up on me?" Serena repeated.

"Do I need your permission before I call my own home?" he retorted sharply.

"No, any more than I need your permission before I can see my friends."

"It would be better for you if that man were not your friend," he said somberly. "Be warned, and if you ignore the warning, at least have the decency not to flaunt yourself with him on these premises."

"Now look—" Serena started to say, but checked herself as the door was flung open and Louisa burst excitedly into the room. In the same movement Serena and Carlo took a step back from each other, trying to hide their flushed faces and hot, angry eyes. "Oh Serena, I'm so glad you're here," Louisa said, hugging her. "You're in time for the big test, and it's the most thrilling of all."

"Is it, darling?" she said, striving to sound normal. "What's going to happen?"

"Papa's going to drive the car at three hundred kilometers an hour," Louisa declared triumphantly.

"But—this isn't a racing car?" Serena queried.

"No, it isn't," Carlo said. Although he was still pale, he'd regained his composure. "But the man in the street likes his cars manufactured to go fast, even if he can't actually use the speed."

"The man in the streets can't afford a Valetti," Serena pointed out wryly. "You need to be a millionaire to pay a hundred thousand pounds for a car."

"You seem very well informed," Carlo observed, giving her a sudden keen look, "but a little out-of-date.

The *last* model was a hundred thousand pounds. This new one will be a hundred and twenty thousand.''

Serena shrugged as if to say that she was equally uninterested either way, but she guessed she'd given away something about herself. She was sure of it when Carlo said significantly, "Have you ever ridden in a Valetti sports car, Serena?"

"The nearest I've ever been to one was the other side of a rope at the London Motor Show," she said, and no effort could quite keep the hint of wistfulness from her voice.

And Carlo was a devil. He knew just what to say to demolish her defenses. "Would you like to ride with me?" he asked now, his eyes on her.

She fought to hang on to her dignity, but it was useless, and she heard the longing words, "Do you mean it?" burst from her own lips.

Carlo lifted his phone and spoke a few commanding words in Italian. "Papa is calling Erica," Louisa explained. "She's a mechanic."

"She also does some test driving for me," Carlo added, replacing the receiver. "For this she wears racing overalls, and she's going to bring you some."

Erica appeared a few moments later. She was a dark-haired young woman with a slim, elegant figure, roughly the same size as Serena's. "Bring Signora Fletcher to me when she's ready," Carlo ordered, and left the office, his hand on Louisa's shoulder.

"You can leave your clothes in here," Erica said, opening a door that led from the office into an austere bedroom, furnished with only a bed, a chest of drawers and a closet. "Signor Valetti sleeps here when the pressure of work is very great."

She took the dress and slip Serena removed and hung them in the closet. "I'd take your tights off as well," she said. "These overalls have three layers, and they're incredibly hot." Serena complied, then stepped into the silky overalls, which zipped up in front, hugging her like a second skin. Her heart was beating with eager anticipation.

Erica led her out of the office and through a maze of buildings until they reached one that looked like an aircraft hangar, near the track. Its wide doors were open, and as Serena approached she saw the car being wheeled out by reverent mechanics.

It was a beautiful creation, low to the ground, with sleek, windswept lines. The doors lifted up and over, revealing a narrow interior into which she must slide. Checking the speedometer, she gave a little gasp as she saw that it really did go up to three hundred kilometres. There was a parallel dial, giving the miles. "One hundred and eighty-six miles an hour," she murmured, astounded.

Carlo glanced up. "Getting cold feet? You can back out if you like."

"Not a chance," she said firmly.

"Have you ever gone so fast before?"

"Never. I'm looking forward to it."

He spoke seriously. "Don't think of it as simply speeding. It's a new dimension, a new world. Like traveling in time. It's beyond description."

"Then what are we waiting for?" she asked.

He did a brief check of the car before climbing nimbly inside and indicating for Serena to get in beside him. She did so, sliding down into the space, which enclosed her like a womb. The engine purred silkily to life and the sound made her give a sigh of pure satisfaction. Carlo laughed with an exultant note she'd never heard him use before. "Yes, it's beautiful. You could lull a baby to sleep with it."

He swung onto the track, and as soon as the road was clear ahead of them, Serena felt a push in the small of her back and the car shot forward. She immediately had the sensation of speed, but realized it must come from being so close to the ground, for the speedometer registered only seventy miles an hour. As she looked at it the needle began to climb—eighty, ninety, a hundred, a hundred and ten.

She stole a glance at Carlo. His voice had revealed how proud he was of this silky beauty and smooth seamless motion, but he sat impassive, his hands resting lightly on the wheel, controlling the machine with the merest touch.

She looked at the speedometer again, and gulped. Almost without her knowing it they'd climbed to a hundred and twenty. Before her eyes the needle glided up another ten—another—and then another. They were doing a hundred and fifty.

A brick wall appeared up ahead. They were traveling straight for it. Serena's eyes widened and she waited for the inevitable crash. But at the last minute the wall was snatched out of their path. She tried to think how fast a man would have to react before he could take a corner at this speed, but it made her giddy.

Then Carlo said quietly, "Are you ready?"

"For anything," she said with more firmness than she felt.

She thought she heard him laugh, but it was hard to be sure because the next moment they were shooting forward and the needle was soaring purposefully toward the hundred-and-eighty-six mark. As it reached

ON HIS HONOR   129

the top, Serena found that the world was streaming past too fast for her to distinguish individual objects. Everything outside the car blurred into a haze, leaving them isolated, alone together. Carlo showed neither apprehension nor excitement, as though to move at this hair-raising pace was the most natural thing in the world. But for him it *was* natural. This was his element. The hands rested on the wheel with the lightest of touches, gentle but absolutely in control.

Suddenly she remembered his hands on another occasion. Then, too, they had been gentle, eliciting a response with the softest touch. In the same moment she became aware of the heat of the overalls that enclosed her from neck to ankles. The thrumming of the engine pervaded her through her feet, her calves, her thighs, her loins. She'd lost the sensation of speed. Only the outside world was going fast. Here inside, everything was happening very slowly.

She turned her head to drink in the details of his face, and as if a light had come on in her brain she saw for the first time the contrast between the harsh jaw angle and the curve of his lower lip with its hint of vulnerability. She'd known his mouth hardened by anger or cold irony, but she'd also known it touching her with tenderness and passion. Time was going at its own speed in this enclosed world that held only themselves, and in that mysterious speed it seemed that two separate moments could be present together. For his lips were on hers again, caressing them purposefully until she welcomed him, and his eyes, fixed intently on the road, somehow shone down joyfully into hers.

The heat flooding through her was the heat of their mutual passion; the soft pounding from the engine was the blood thrumming through her veins as she moved in

rhythm to its urging, wanting him, craving the feel of
him against the tender skin of her inner thighs, and then
deeper, deeper into her willing body, piercing sweet and
beautiful. Somehow the separate strands of time had
become one, so that at the moment she felt him claim
her, she fixed her eyes on him sitting beside her in the
car, not touching her, not looking at her, but aware of
her with every inch of his body.

They were losing speed. The outside world came into
existence again as they slowed to a halt. As the engine
died, the silence grew deafening. Slowly Carlo met her
eyes and held them for a long moment, his breath coming raggedly. A mechanic tried to pull open his door but
Carlo clamped his hand on it, refusing to allow anyone
to intrude on them. Still looking at her, he touched a
switch, bringing the engine back to life and turned the
car back out of the hangar, letting it glide until they
reached the door of his office.

He got out and came around to raise her door, giving her his hand to help her out. It was only when she
set foot on the ground that she discovered she was
shaking and her bones seemed to have turned to jelly.
Carlo caught her as she staggered, lifted her in his arms
and kicked open the door of the office. Once inside he
went straight into the bedroom and set her on her feet.
But he kept hold of her to stop her legs from buckling.

Serena was on fire with urgency. She craved him as
she'd never craved anything before in her life, and that
craving swamped caution. Scarcely knowing what she
did, she pulled at the zip of his overalls and the material parted, revealing the thick, curly hair of his chest,
and she laid her face against it with a sigh of satisfaction. Through the hair she could feel that his flesh was
burning like her own, and beneath that his heart thun-

dered with the same slow rhythm that possessed her body.

Then Carlo grasped her shoulders and thrust her a few inches back so that he could look down into her flushed face. His own look was wild and his eyes glittered. But he didn't move, and for a terrible moment she feared he might reject her. His fingers dug into her shoulders, and she could feel him shaking with the struggle going on within him. Then he gave a groan that seemed to be torn from his depths and crushed her against him, kissing her with all the fierceness of a man maddened by his own desires. She could sense the fury in his lips, could tell from the trembling of his hard body that he hadn't abandoned the fight against her, but that he was losing, and knew it.

At last his hands released her, but his eyes didn't. Without taking his gaze from her he took a step back, reached behind him and locked the door. He took hold of the zipper in front of her overalls, opening it slowly, still watching her as if hypnotized. When it was open he seized the collar with both hands and pushed the material back around her shoulders, pulling the coveralls down so that she was naked to the waist, then put his hands behind her to draw her against his chest. Looking up, Serena saw in his face everything he couldn't hide, his aching desire for her, his scorn for his own weakness, and something else that might have been love or hate. She was past caring. There was a soft, urgent throbbing between her legs that only he could satisfy. He belonged there, and she was determined to have him.

He began to kiss the base of her throat with hot, demanding lips, making flickering forays with his tongue that sent forks of lightning through her. She freed her hands quickly from the sleeves of her overall and clasped them behind his head, twining her fingers through his thick, dark hair. It was glorious, but it wasn't enough. He was her man, hers in the deepest way a man could belong to a woman, and she wanted far more than this. She seized one of his hands and laid it over her breast, arching against him to let him know what she wanted.

Through the haze of desire that enveloped her she was vaguely aware of him turning so that he could sit on the bed and draw her close. His lips enfolded one nipple and she groaned at the dizzying sensation.

His hands met behind her back, slid lower until they were inside her overalls, and curved to cup her buttocks in his palm. He looked up at her and she saw his face suffused with desire and the same madness that consumed herself. In a fever Carlo rose and stripped off his own overalls, revealing the proud manhood that was ready for her.

Their first union had been poetic and full of tender beauty. This was different. This was the slaking of raw, powerful, physical need. They had the intimate knowledge of people whose flesh had once been united in a blaze of ecstatic glory, and such knowledge could never be forgotten. The memory of it had lingered through weeks of enmity, tormenting them until neither of them could endure it any longer. Now nothing else mattered but to be one again.

The narrow bed barely had room for them both, but he immediately covered her with his body, and when she parted her legs in urgent invitation, he drove into her with vigor but no subtlety. Serena let out a gasping groan at how good it felt and immediately clasped her arms behind him. She felt herself consumed by heat. The excitement streaming through her was like the glow of a furnace as the coals turned from red to gold. Carlo's sheer strength was exhilarating. His arms held her in an unbreakable embrace, the muscles of his back were hard beneath her hands, and the steely power of his loins pierced her to the quick, again and again, so that a series of shuddering cries escaped her as the heat mounted and the gleaming gold turned to white. They were caught up in the furnace together, searing, melting, uniting.

And when she thought it was over it had hardly begun, for his passion was barely slaked, and he was still there between her legs, in her body, affirming and reaffirming himself in her. He moved slowly now, drawing out each exquisite, beautiful, torturing movement to the last moment, then thrust deep into the heart of her secret self, again slowly and with a combination of control and abandon that took her breath away.

Her body convulsed in the rhythm that he commanded. The pleasure was sending her out of her mind, and in that fevered craziness she wasn't herself anymore but a part of Carlo; yet not Carlo as she knew him, but a different man whose eyes glowed into hers, eliciting from her an equally fierce and passionate answer. When he claimed her it was all bittersweet delight, spreading out through her flesh to her fingertips so that there was not one inch of her that wasn't singing with pleasure.

She was caught in a spiral that reeled giddily upward to heights she had only glimpsed before, never touched. But this time there was no stopping, and together they spun off into space. Now the ecstasy was there for the taking, and she grasped it eagerly, feeling it fall gloriously into her hands. Yet somehow it was impossible to grasp, and in despair she felt it slip through her fingers, to dissolve into nothing.

It was over, and they were their everyday selves again, for whatever of good or evil, joy or misery they could bring each other.

Nine

Carlo found himself lying on the narrow bed, his arm about Serena, who was cramped up against him by the wall. If the perfect communion of their flesh had been reflected in their hearts, this would have been the perfect position, but as his sanity returned Carlo wanted to groan with horror at what he'd revealed. When he'd desired her, she'd rejected him cruelly. But at the first snap of her fingers she'd enticed him back into her arms. She'd proven she could do as she liked with him, and that knowledge would always be between them.

He didn't dare to look at her for fear of the amusement and contempt he would see in her eyes. But she couldn't scorn him any more than he scorned himself for his weakness. Moving gingerly, he disentangled himself from her and swung his legs over the side of the bed. "Well," he said in the most cynical voice he could assume, "have you made up your mind which of us was using the other?" To his vast relief his voice hadn't shaken. He was shaking inside.

There was a short silence before Serena said, "Oh, I think it was about a draw this time. Neither of us expected anything else, surely?"

He was pulling his overalls up as far as his waist. Now he turned to face her and found her looking up at him with a cool smile on her face, a picture of composure, when only a moment ago...

"Naturally not," he returned. "Our battle lines are pretty clear by now."

He returned to shrugging himself into the sleeves. Serena sat very still, her heart pounding. She kept her smile in place by an effort of will, thankful that he'd spoken before she'd had time to utter the words of love that had risen to her lips. But the pain of having her love cast back at her, even though Carlo didn't know he was doing it, was so great that for a moment she hated him.

She got up and dressed hurriedly. All she wanted now was to get away from him. But suddenly he turned on her and said harshly, "Why the devil don't you get out?"

"You mean—?"

"Go back to England."

"And leave Louisa with you?"

"Why not? I'm her father."

She seemed to see a red mist before her eyes, made up of hate and despair. And before she could stop them, the terrible words were out. "But you're not her father. Louisa isn't your child."

She held her breath, waiting for the explosion, or perhaps the jeering disbelief. Instead, she realized Carlo was looking at her with his head slightly on one side, and an ironic twist to his lips. "So," he said at last, "you do know. I've been wondering."

"You mean—*you* know?" she stammered, staring at him in disbelief.

"Of course. I've known for two years."

She sat down on the bed. "But—how?"

He gave a mirthless crack of laughter. "How do you think? Dawn told me in a moment of spite. She had a lot of those. That was how I usually found out what she was up to. We had a quarrel and she blurted it out for the pleasure of hurting me—just like you did."

She stared. "What did you do?" she asked.

"I walked out, swearing I never wanted to see either of them again. But when I came to my senses, I realized I had to accept it. Louisa and I love each other. That's more important than Dawn's vindictive need to hurt me—" he looked at her significantly "—or yours."

She drew a deep breath, trying to come to terms with this shattering discovery. Dawn had told her that Carlo didn't know the truth, but she'd lied. Her adored Dawn had lied, and about something so important. What else had she lied about?

"When did she tell you?" Carlo asked quietly.

"When she was dying. She said you didn't know." Suddenly overwhelmed, Serena dropped her head into her hands. Carlo sat on the bed beside her. "Serena," he said, "haven't you realized yet that you didn't really know Dawn at all?"

"I'm beginning to realize it," she admitted. "But since I came here there have been so many things—just details, but they added up—and the way Primo spoke of her." She looked up quickly, "Is he—?"

"Louisa's father? Yes." His mouth twisted. "Dawn got a special kick out of telling me that. Haven't you seen how like Primo she is, not in looks but in her way of taking risks without thinking of the consequences. He'll end by killing himself, and so will Louisa—if I don't stop her."

"Surely she'll have to know the truth one day?"

"What truth?" he demanded with soft violence. "She's my daughter because I love and care for her. *That's* the truth. It's the only truth she's ever going to hear from me or anyone else, including you."

"Can you carry that through for the rest of her life?" Serena demanded.

"I can do whatever I set my mind to. I set my mind to this two years ago, and I haven't looked back. Nor will I." His eyes narrowed. "Are you going to be the one to cross me?"

Serena shook her head, awed by the depths of generosity that could make a man do this. She wanted to reach out to Carlo and tell him how deeply he'd touched her heart, but while she was seeking the right words, he walked to the door. "I'm glad that's understood," he said curtly. "Now I must be going. I've wasted far too much time."

Serena didn't even try to sleep that night. She knew there would be no rest for her until she'd come to terms with the shattering discovery she'd made that afternoon: not just that Carlo had known about Louisa all the time, but that Dawn had lied to her.

She tried to argue it away, to say that Dawn hadn't known what she was saying, but it didn't work. Ever since she'd arrived here there'd been hints that her cousin had been different from the picture she'd cherished, and now those hints came together in one irresistible truth. Dawn had deceived her, and she had deceived herself.

Most of all she'd been blind about Carlo. She'd thought so many terrible things about him, but the truth was that he had the greatness of heart to accept another man's child rather than hurt a little girl. Carlo had caused a flowering within her. She'd lain in his arms, in the searing delight of passion given and fulfilled. Their lovemaking had been not merely the satiation of physical desire but an expression of the most profound emotion of her life. She'd refused to admit to herself that she loved him, but now there was no longer any need to refuse, and in the privacy of her own heart she gladly confessed her love. And yet, she now realized, she knew nothing about the kind of man he was. His feelings toward her remained a secret, perhaps even from himself.

For hours she paced the floor, unwilling to go to bed, because she knew she would only stare at the ceiling. Summer had arrived and suddenly her bedroom seemed hot and airless. She threw open the window and stood looking out into the distance, where she could still see some of the lights of Rome. Her skin was burning with the memory of the passionate encounter earlier that day. Carlo had touched her everywhere, and every inch of her remembered him, and wanted him. If only he was here with her now, and in the hot darkness they could rediscover each other, without the lies that had held them apart. She listened tensely, hoping to hear some sound that would herald his arrival, but there was only deep, intense silence of the night.

But then she did hear something. It seemed to reach her through the window, and she leaned out, holding herself very still. At last she heard it again—the sound of weeping, coming out the window of Louisa's room next door.

Serena sped across the floor, out into the corridor, and into the blue-and-white bedroom where Louisa slept. There was no doubt about it now. Louisa was crying, but doing so in a way Serena had never seen a child cry before. She was muffling her sobs in the pillow that she clutched tightly to her with both arms, but she couldn't completely silence the terrible storm of grief that shook her. Serena touched the little shoulders and felt them shudder with the violence of the emotion that possessed the child. "Louisa," she whispered, "Louisa...I'm here."

She tried to gather her into her arms, but Louisa burrowed deeper into the pillow and wept even more bitterly. Serena could make out only one word. "Papa...Papa..." repeated over and over.

Serena wasted no more time but ran out of the room and along the corridor until she came to the door to Carlo's bedroom. She hesitated only a moment before turning the handle and hurrying in. The room was lighted by a small lamp, revealing that the bed was empty. Then she saw him standing by the window in pajamas and dressing gown, his shoulders hunched, his head sunk in brooding melancholy. He turned swiftly when he heard her, and she saw that his face was haggard, his hair tousled, and he looked younger and more vulnerable than she had ever seen him. At the same moment she became aware that she hadn't stopped to put on a robe, and her nightdress was revealing. She clasped her hands over her breasts. "Come quickly," she urged. "It's Louisa. Something's terribly wrong."

He was out of the door before she'd finished speaking, racing along the corridor and into Louisa's room.

He stared in horror at the child, still huddled in the same position, before dropping to one knee beside the bed and trying to take her in his arms. But she shrank away from him.

"*Piccina,*" he said gently. "Come to your Papa."

"No, no," she wept frantically. She began to gabble something in Italian. Serena couldn't catch it, but Carlo heard and she saw him flinch.

He pulled the little girl into his arms, cradling her against his shoulder. She had no more strength to fight him, but sat there, whispering out her grief, hiccuping between words.

At last Carlo raised his head and said to Serena. "Louisa overheard a couple of mechanics talking this afternoon. She's got some crazy idea that I'm not her father. Of course, it's all a misunderstanding." He was watching Serena over Louisa's head, his eyes deadly. "It's a misunderstanding, isn't it?" he repeated emphatically.

Serena heard herself say, "Of course it is."

"No, no," Louisa wept. "They said—"

"Whatever they said, they're wrong," Carlo interrupted her firmly. "Of course you're mine, *piccina*. You've always been mine and you always will be. We're going to stay together and love each other for ever and ever."

But Louisa shook her head. "They heard you and Serena talking today—at the track—you said you'd always known you weren't my real papa—"

"I didn't say that," Carlo said at once. "I said I'd always found it hard to believe I could be your father, because no man could be as lucky as to have a daughter like you. You're my miracle, *piccina*. I give thanks for you every day, because you're sweet and loving, but most of all because you're *mine.*''

Louisa became very still. The other two held their breath, sensing that she was struggling inside herself, trying to know whether to believe this.

''It's true, my darling,'' Serena said urgently.

Louisa raised her head from her father's shoulder and looked at Serena through her tears. ''*You* say so?'' she whispered.

''Yes.'' Serena sank onto the bed beside the other two, knowing what she had to do. ''This is your father, and he loves you more than anyone in the world. Nothing can ever change that.''

Louisa's gaze was fixed on her. ''You promise me that what you say is true?'' she said. ''On your honor?''

''I promise you, on my honor, that what I say is true.''

Louisa gave a little sigh and put her arms contentedly around Carlo's neck, plainly having had the reassurance she needed. Carlo enfolded her in his strong arms and the two held each other in silence. Serena slipped quietly out to her own room. There was a lump in her throat at what she'd seen. Carlo's love for the little girl shone bright and clear, dimming every other aspect of the dreadful story.

At last there came a knock on her door. She opened it and stood back to let him pass. ''Is she all right?''

Before answering he moved swiftly to close the window. ''I'm taking no chances on her hearing more,'' he said. ''I left her asleep. She seems content now.'' He stared at her. ''She's content because *you* reassured her. She believes I'm telling the truth because *you* backed me up,'' he said in a baffled, angry voice.

"I can't explain that, except that Louisa and I have been on the same wavelength from the start."

"Meaning that she and I are not?"

"No, I never meant—"

"Listen, while I tell you something," he interrupted her, his eyes kindling. "Louisa is *my* daughter in every way that matters. To hell with Primo Viareggi. *I* taught her to walk, I calmed her fears when she had nightmares, I talked to her teachers and took her out on her birthdays, I did. Not her mother, who was usually off doing something else, but me. That's what makes her mine. That's why I fought you with every weapon I could lay my hands on and didn't give a damn how unscrupulous I had to be."

"I know that," she said, very pale. "I can't even blame you anymore. I never dreamed she loved you that much. If I had, I'd never have tried to take her away from you."

"But you have taken her away from me, in some way that I can't define. She barely knows you, but after all Louisa and I have shared, she gives her confidence to you. *Why?*"

"Perhaps because I'm a woman and a little girl needs a mother. You're a wonderful father to her, I can see that, but she needs more."

"And that's the biggest joke of all, if she only knew it, because you're the one who caused her all this pain. You broke her heart by dragging up something she should never have suspected. Damn you for your interference!"

"Carlo, I'm sorry, I really am. If you'll only—"

"Don't ask me to forgive you, because you'll ask in vain," he said bleakly. "I never forgive anyone who hurts my child."

She passed a hand over her eyes. "I can understand your feeling like that. But there's nothing I wouldn't do to put it right."

He looked at her strangely. "Do you really mean that?"

"Of course I mean it. Whatever that little girl needs, I'll give to her, if it's in my power."

"But you know what she needs," he said, still giving her an odd look. "You've just said it. She needs a mother."

"But—"

"And you're the mother she's chosen. It's very simple. The sooner we get married, the better."

"*Get married?* Are you out of your mind?"

"Far from it. I'm doing what's necessary to protect my daughter."

"But you hate me," she said, watching his eyes.

His grin was without warmth. "Well, that's more or less mutual. We both know that. But I have to keep you here because you're dangerous. You know my secret, so I want you where I can watch you. Louisa loves you. Heaven knows why, but she does. She's lost one mother and I'm going to make certain she doesn't lose another. And this way I can be sure you'll keep quiet. If you try to make trouble I'll do whatever is required to silence you."

"Don't threaten me," Serena snapped.

"Threats are the only language your family understands. I learned that once before. I was nice to Dawn and she flung it back in my face. Now the days of being nice are over. I'm not asking you, I'm *telling* you— we're getting married."

"You must be mad."

"Yes," he agreed without hesitation. "As mad as this."

Before she knew what he meant to do, he'd pulled her into his arms and was kissing her ruthlessly. His lips were hard and insistent as they moved over hers, and the arms that held her were like steel. She could feel no tenderness in him, only fury, and her soul rose in rebellion. "Do you think this is the way to persuade me?" she gasped.

"I'm not persuading you," he grated. "The decision's been taken. You don't know yet how determined I can be, so don't force me to show you. Just take my word for it that we're going to be married." In the dim light his face hung above her, his eyes glittering. "It needn't be a bad marriage, Serena. After all, we have one thing that unites us, don't we?"

He dropped his head again and began inflicting sweet torture on the soft skin just below her ear. She gasped at the sensation. She was still angry with him, but no anger could subdue the pleasure that rioted through her at the flickering movements of his tongue. "Don't we?" he insisted in a hoarse murmur.

"Yes... yes..." she whispered wildly.

Her mind cried out that this was all wrong. She was being swept away by a desire that overwhelmed her, silencing all reason. Logic told her that she was crazy to consider this marriage, but logic had no place in the mad clamor of the senses that possessed her now. When he picked her up and carried her to the bed she instinctively put her arms around his neck. As he lay down beside her she was ready for him. It was only a few hours since they'd been together, but he was as fiery and vigorous as though it had been months. She gave him back fire for fire, claiming him fiercely, and when their moment came it was possible to believe that this would be enough to see them through the years.

But when it was over he got up and left her, and she knew that, whatever they had, it was incomplete. Today she'd discovered a new side to him, but it had been revealed not to her, but to the little girl who had his love. With Louisa he'd shown all the gentle, protective tenderness of which he was capable. As she lay alone in the darkness, her body throbbing with the aftermath of fulfillment and her heart aching with loneliness, Serena knew that Carlo's love was the lodestar that drew her on, and she would never know peace until she reached home.

Ten

The wedding was set to take place in a month, and as quietly as could be managed. The person most pleased was Louisa, who was transformed with joy at the prospect of keeping Serena with her forever. When Serena promised her that she could be a bridesmaid at last, she let out a piercing shriek of excitement. Carlo flinched and covered his ears, but his eyes were smiling. Later he said quietly to Serena, "Thank you." If they had a common purpose it was to keep Louisa happy, and in putting on a good front for her they overcame some awkwardness with each other.

Shopping for her wedding dress wasn't easy. Thoughts of that other wedding dress came back to her, along with the memory of Carlo turning away with a look of distaste. She had no idea of how he wanted her to look, and she was too shy to discuss it with him.

She returned home one day, after a tiring and unsatisfying shopping trip. It was a relief to be back in the cool of the villa. Then, as she moved through the hall into the garden, she heard a voice that made a tremor go through her. It was the husky voice of the well-preserved beauty she had seen Carlo lunching with, and she wondered, incredulously, if he'd actually invited the woman to his wedding.

As soon as Serena stepped into the garden, she recognized her. She was sitting on the stone terrace, one long, beautiful leg crossed over the other and swinging negligently. She had the slender figure of a girl, and a face that still looked almost young. But at any age she would have been a ravishing beauty, and her presence gave Serena a stab of anger. Or was it alarm?

The boy whose face was so like Carlo's was there, too. The woman had her hand on his arm, and they were both laughing with Carlo, who was smiling down on them both. The three of them made a perfect picture of a happy family.

Then Carlo looked up, saw her and broke off the conversation to say, "Serena, come here and meet my mother."

Serena looked around for anyone who could possibly be his mother, but without success. At the sight of her total bewilderment the woman broke into a gale of laughter, and advanced toward her, arms outstretched, saying, "Oh *cara*, I love you already for not knowing it was me."

"You—are Carlo's mother?" Serena said, astonished.

"*Si*, and all the diets and the exercise, and the scandalous bills from the surgeon who does my face, you made them all worthwhile," the woman declared.

"Carlo, I adore your new wife." She kissed Serena warmly. "My name is Gita, and this is my son, Tomaso." She brought forward the boy, who shyly offered his hand.

Serena made a hasty effort to collect her scattered wits. "You didn't tell me you had a brother," she reproved Carlo.

"Half brother," he said smiling. "Tomaso is from Gita's second marriage."

Now Serena could detect the resemblance between Carlo and his mother. It was elusive, because Gita's face had been extensively remodeled, but it was there, and Tomaso shared it, hence the startling similarity between him and Carlo that had caused her so much anguish. She wanted to laugh aloud with happiness and relief.

Louisa joined them. She was at ease with both Gita and Tomaso, whom she called "Uncle" in a spirit of mischief. Supper was a cheerful meal. Gita came down in a resplendent evening dress that made Serena feel like a provincial dowdy.

When the meal was over and the children had been sent to bed, Gita declared that she must go and talk to Valeria in the kitchen. "There is a recipe she promised me," she said, "and besides, you must be alone together when Carlo tells you of the wonderfully romantic wedding gift he is preparing for you." She departed in a flurry of silk chiffon.

Carlo cleared his throat, and it seemed to Serena that he was embarrassed. "My mother is an eternal romantic," he said. "She likes to see moonlight and roses everywhere."

"From which I take it that your wedding gift isn't romantic at all," Serena said lightly. There was an ache of disappointed hope in her heart, but she was getting used to that.

"Let's say it's primarily a good publicity move," Carlo responded. "I've decided to call the new sports car the *Serena*. The press love the idea."

Despite knowing that it meant nothing, her heart leapt briefly. It would have been such a lovely compliment. "You've already put out a press release?"

"Not yet, but there's been a leak. My staff at the track have been telling the story of how we got engaged within a few hours of our drive. The story is that I asked you to marry me when we were doing top speed."

She took her cue from his dry tone and said, with a fair imitation of amusement, "How on earth do they imagine you accomplished that and controlled the car?"

"It's incredible, isn't it? I knew you'd appreciate the joke. By the way, I've managed to pinpoint the employees who listened to our conversation and passed it on. They'll be dismissed tomorrow."

"That isn't wise," Serena said at once.

"What?" His eyes flashed.

"If you dismiss them they'll have a grievance, and they'll know there's something in what they heard."

He frowned, and she knew he'd taken her point. "What do you suggest then?" he said at last.

"Find them alternative employment a long way away. I'm sure you can manage it."

"You're right. That's a much better solution. I can see I'm marrying a wise woman." He smiled and lifted his glass courteously toward her.

These days it was always like this if they happened to be alone. Carlo was polite, even charming, but he'd retired behind a barrier and she couldn't reach him. To turn the conversation, Serena said, "I think your mother's a marvel."

"She's incredible, isn't she?" he agreed at once.

"You've kept her very quiet."

He shrugged. "We seldom see each other. She left my father twenty years ago. Now she's married to an industrialist in Milan."

"How old were you when she went away?"

"About twelve—if it matters."

Refusing to be put off by the sudden chill in his voice, Serena persisted, "Of course it matters. It must have affected you, being abandoned by your mother when you were twelve."

"She didn't abandon me," he said quickly. "I understood her reasons perfectly."

"At *twelve?*"

He gave a wintry smile. "In my father's house a child grew up very quickly. And as you can see, we have an excellent relationship now. Everything is forgiven and forgotten."

"That's not true," Serena said at once.

"What do you mean?" he asked sharply.

"You haven't really forgiven her. You just try to believe that you have. But you keep her picture hidden. I found it by accident one day in your office. Why don't you put it on show?"

He shrugged. "I must have forgotten." The air was suddenly crackling with tension. "Does it matter?"

"I suppose not," she said, letting it go. "I just wanted to tell you how much I like her. I think I'll ask her to help me choose my wedding dress. I'm worn out with looking and not being able to make up my mind."

"Do you remember your other wedding dress?" he asked suddenly.

"Yes." She flushed slightly. "You hated me in it."

"No. I hated *it* on *you*. It was so garish against your simplicity. I wanted you in the colors of nature, so that you looked as if you'd just come out of the woods, with your hair long and braided with flowers."

He stopped and seemed to emerge from a dream. "I'm sure whatever you choose will be delightful," he said politely. "Shall we find my mother now?"

Gita took her over for the rest of the evening and set herself to charm her future daughter-in-law. She did it very thoroughly, for she was an expert, but nonetheless Serena had an odd sense of distance. Gita seemed to exert herself automatically, as if it was vital to her that everyone love her. She insisted Serena must call her Gita, as Carlo did. "Mama sounds so old," she said with a pretty laugh. Even Louisa called her by her first name, at Gita's insistence.

By the end of the evening they were on sufficiently good terms for Serena to ask for help with the wedding dress. They were alone in Gita's room, and she described how Carlo wanted her to look, without speaking of what she'd seen on his face at that moment.

Gita nodded. "Behind his stern appearance my son is a romantic," she observed with satisfaction. "I know where to take you. A shop where they contrive great simplicity at enormous expense." Then, apparently recalling that Serena didn't come from a monied family, she added, "It will be my gift."

"Thank you, but I can afford it," Serena said with a smile. "I've just sold the house in England that used to belong to my grandparents."

She had, in fact, dallied over the sale until the last minute, unwilling to let the happy place go. But the agent had called two weeks ago to say the buyer was getting impatient, and she'd agreed because she didn't want to depend totally on Carlo's money. She'd tried to reject the settlement he'd made on her, but given up when she saw that she was insulting him. Instead she insisted that he cut the amount to a quarter. He'd been furious, but he'd yielded.

Next day Gita took her to the Via Condotti, the most elegant and costly street in all Rome. She gave some commands in rapid Italian and a series of dresses was produced. The first and second weren't quite right, but Serena took one look at the third and fell in love. It was cut on deceptively simple lines, and made of cream silk with a delicate pattern of embroidered leaves. When she tried it on she knew that this dress was as right as the other, glittering dress, five years ago, had been wrong. And this marriage too was right, for she was marrying the man she loved, and one day she might dare to tell him.

Two days before the wedding, the Valetti *Serena* was unveiled to the press, and in a ceremony lighted by a thousand flashbulbs, Carlo Valetti proudly presented his fiancée with her wedding gift—the first model off the production line. It was a splendid public relations coup.

The wedding was more private, taking place in the small chapel belonging to the villa. Serena walked slowly down the aisle, the soft dress swinging about her ankles, her flowing hair adorned with the fresh flowers that Gita had arranged to be delivered that morning, and matching flowers in her hand. Louisa, a bridesmaid at last, concentrated intently on keeping in step behind her.

But Serena had no attention for anyone but Carlo. Her eyes were on his face as she slowly approached him, and although his expression didn't change, she sensed a softening in the harsh lines and around his eyes, and the instincts that had flowered with her love told her that he was pleased. She reached out to lay her hand on his, and within half an hour she was his wife.

Afterward there was a reception at which most of the guests were racing people. The bride and groom left early to fly to Paris, where they would stay for only three days before traveling south to Provence so that they wouldn't miss the French Grand Prix.

"Do you mind about that?" Carlo asked her as he poured champagne in their hotel room that night.

"Not at all. I think it's all been splendidly organized," she said, smiling.

"You *do* mind. I don't blame you. But let's see how you feel when I've given you your wedding gift."

"But I've had that."

"No, that was just for the press."

"You mean I don't get to keep the car?" she asked in genuine dismay, for despite her disappointment at the PR aspects, she'd lost her heart to the beautiful vehicle.

He grinned. "No, the car's yours. You've got the papers to prove it. But I have another set of papers to give you." He took out a large envelope and handed it to her. Puzzled, Serena plunged inside and drew out some documents. Then her eyes opened wide.

She was holding the title deeds to her old home.

"It was *you,*" she breathed. "The agent told me it was being bought by a company."

"I hid behind a company to surprise you," he said, smiling. "I told you I didn't like it being sold. I've been negotiating to buy it for weeks, but you kept putting it off."

"I didn't want to sell it."

"Good. We'll keep it and take Louisa back there one day."

Serena pressed her lips to the title deeds in a surge of joy. Here was the gleam of affection she'd searched for in the chilly formality of her wedding. "Do you remember the day I told you that it was a place I loved?" Carlo asked.

"Yes." She smiled, but then a shadow crossed her face at the memory of happiness that had ended in bitterness. He saw it and understood.

"There are things about that day that are best forgotten if we're to live together in peace," he said. "But there were other things..." He hesitated and she could hear his breath coming raggedly. "There were other things..."

"Yes," she whispered, looking at him. "There were other things..."

He took gentle hold of the lacy peignoir and slipped it from her shoulders, revealing the low-cut silk nightgown. Her heart was racing madly at the look in his eyes and the touch of his fingers drifting down her arms.

"Serena," he said slowly, "let us remember only the good things tonight."

"And—tomorrow?" she couldn't help asking.

He gave a faint smile. "Who knows? Tomorrow we may be enemies again. But tonight—" a shudder seemed to go through him as he drew her close "—tonight let there be only this." He laid his mouth over hers, and suddenly all thought became impossible in the shimmering excitement that flowed through her. This was the first time he'd held her in his arms since the night they'd decided to marry, and her flesh had yearned for him as fiercely as her heart.

Her filmy nightgown slipped to the floor. She immediately began work on his pajamas, not stopping until she'd tossed them aside and he was as naked as herself. At once they both realized that they had to make love immediately, this very minute. Neither knew who made the first move toward the bed, but they were there, pulling each other down, feverishly kissing and caressing to reach the moment when there could be no more questions and only one certainty. As she enveloped him in herself, Serena felt a sense of desperate relief that at least they still had this to live on until she could find the way to his heart. He couldn't resist her, and he knew it. Perhaps he even resented it. But as long as it was true, the dice weren't completely loaded against her.

As they parted she saw the wary look return to his eyes, but she ignored it and took a gamble. For the first time they were together in a bed that was large enough for them to savor each other at leisure, and that was what she meant to do. For all their frantic passion, she'd never enjoyed the luxury of simply considering his strong, lean body. Now she pushed him gently onto his back and sat up, turning to face him, and keeping her hand on his chest, softly kneaded and teased him. He didn't speak but his eyes were fixed on her, and his breathing was unsteady.

She watched his face through the strands of her tousled hair as she let her hand drift down his chest to the flat stomach and narrow hips, making whorls on the skin with her fingertips. A soft groan broke from him. "You look like a wood sprite, sitting there," he whispered, "half human and half elf."

She moved her hand softly again, and smiled at what she discovered. Despite the vigor of their first mating he was already proudly erect. "What are you doing to me, elf?" he asked hoarsely.

"Whatever you like," she said softly.

He reached up both hands to cup her breasts, caressing them with fingers and thumbs until her loins throbbed with need of him and she was gasping. She threw her head back, but he twined his fingers in her hair and pulled her gently forward to kiss him.

It was her kiss, her tongue in his mouth, exploring and challenging him, and he knew it. To have a woman take control and make love to him, exciting him with tenderness and passion, and a deep understanding of his sensual nature, was a new experience for him. Somewhere in the deep recesses of his mind, he knew he found it alarming, for it demanded a trust he found almost impossible. But it was too late to think of that now. His body, as eager as his mind was reluctant, was responding helplessly to her seductive spell. He was hers, and he had sworn not to be. If he yielded she could use desire to control him, and his pride flinched away from that thought.

Suddenly the unbearable craving she'd ignited in him had to be assuaged. He turned with her in his arms and moved between her legs. The moment when he came into her was like coming home, and he felt himself taken in, welcomed, embraced. Now he could believe that nothing else mattered but to lie with her and be one with her. Together they created something that was more than pleasure, but a kind of kinship with the gods.

But the gods bestowed their favors only to snatch them away, and the moment of loss was cruel, as though the world had suddenly emptied of all joy. If there had been trust between them as well as passion, he could have rested with his head on her breast and let himself be lulled to sleep by the music of her heartbeat. But as joy vanished, the place was filled with caution. He smiled and kissed her, knowing she'd sensed his inner reservation and was hurt by it, but he couldn't help himself.

To his relief she didn't try to stop him when he rose from the bed and went to sit by the window. He stayed there for a long time, until he was sure she was asleep. Then he got quietly back into bed and lay staring into the darkness. Once he rose on one elbow and looked down on her sleeping face. He didn't mean to kiss her, but he found himself doing it, and wondered at the dampness he felt on her cheek.

As soon as they reached Provence for the race, Carlo became involved in technicalities and spent most of his time in the pits. Their physical union was as perfect as it had always been, but Serena saw little of him by day, and when they were together she was acutely aware of barriers that she couldn't pass.

There was an awkward moment when she returned to her hotel to find a huge bouquet of red roses and a note from Primo saying, "I hope you're grateful for my part in your success." She tore it into little pieces, and ordered the flowers removed, but Carlo came in while they were still there and raised his eyebrows.

"It's just Primo being offensive," Serena said.

"Very offensive to send red roses to my wife," Carlo returned curtly. "Was there a note?"

"Yes, but I've torn it up."

"And naturally you're not going to tell me what it said"

"I'm too disgusted with it to repeat it."

A maid arrived to remove the flowers at that moment, and when she'd gone Carlo didn't return to the subject. That night he made love with a fierceness and abandon that had a dangerous edge on it. When she awoke later that night she saw him sitting at the window, every line of his body radiating tension. She spoke his name, and he turned to look at her with the cold eyes of a stranger. The sight struck her dumb, and after a moment he had turned back without speaking.

The next day, to Serena's immense satisfaction, Primo had a poor race and finished fourth. Bernardo, the better of the two Valetti drivers, crossed the finishing line first.

They returned to a boisterous welcome from Louisa, who'd spent the honeymoon visiting Gita, and got back to Rome before them. On the first full day back, Serena announced her intention of trying out her new car.

"You'd better practice on the track until you're used to her," Carlo said. "I'll have it cleared for you today. And be careful. It would be embarrassing if the first *Serena* was smashed up by Serena." His mouth gave a wry twist. "Also, I prefer you alive."

She practiced for two hours on the track, loving the sleek, sweet moving vehicle more every second. That evening, impelled by sheer mischief, she asked, "Am I too old to become a racing driver?" and laughed at the look of alarm on her husband's face.

At moments like that, when his guard slipped a fraction, she felt she might have a chance. But he always recovered quickly, and she found herself once again in an emotional desert, where there was fire and yet, strangely, no warmth.

The racing season continued throughout the summer, with races in different countries every two weeks:

the U.S.A., Canada, France, Britain, Germany. By the time of the Hungarian Grand Prix, Primo was still in the lead in the World Championship table, but he crashed on the fifth lap and his car was a write-off. He escaped unhurt but his lead was slashed. The Valetti cars came in first and second.

"And next month we're going to Monza," Louisa bubbled.

"Next month *you* will be at school," Carlo said with an attempt at firmness.

"Oh *Papa—*"

"Why don't you just give in now?" Serena demanded, amused.

He grinned. "Yes, I might as well."

A week before the race, a vast transporter started the journey north. It contained three cars plus several spare engines, a bewildering collection of different tires and hundreds of spare parts. When it was parked at Monza, it would become the center of the team's efforts, the place where repairs and modifications would be performed away from the eyes of competitors.

Carlo, Serena and Louisa set off the next day and arrived in Monza to find the transporter in place and the team of twenty mechanics already busy. Giulio, the head mechanic, was waiting in the pit. When he'd been introduced to Serena he said seriously, "We may have a problem. Bernardo seems to be going down with some bug. The doctor's with him now."

"Damn!" Carlo exclaimed. "I'd better go over to the hotel and see him."

While he was gone, Serena had a chance to study the fearsome-looking vehicles with their low, windswept bodies, huge engines mounted behind the driving seats, and thick tires mounted on long arms. Carlo returned at last, shaking his head. "Bernardo has the flu. It's not serious but the doctor says he's out of the race."

"But surely you still have Ferrando," Serena said.

"Yes, but he's very much the second driver," Carlo said. "Losing Bernardo is a blow. Why did it have to be here of all places?"

He plunged into discussion with Giulio and after a while, Serena departed and went to do some sightseeing, leaving Louisa with Carlo. She spent a contented afternoon exploring the nearby royal palace, and returned to the hotel to find that Gita and Tomaso had arrived.

"Are you bored out of your mind yet?" Gita asked sympathetically as they relaxed together in her room. She was stretched out on her bed, repairing with a face mask and slices of cucumber the shattering effects of a two-hour journey in an air-conditioned limousine.

"Not bored, exactly. I find cars fascinating. But although my Italian is improving fast, I can't follow the technical discussions," Serena admitted. "I left because I felt in the way."

"Emilio wouldn't let me leave," Gita confided. "He said the boss's wife had to appear fascinated. Heavens, how I came to hate racing. I only come to Monza for Carlo's sake."

"You must know a lot about it," Serena hazarded.

"Much more than I want to," Gita agreed mournfully. "I know that what really matters to Carlo, as it did to his father, is the Constructors' Championship. That's for the most successful make of car. We won't win the drivers' contest. Barring accidents the Neapolitan will get that. But we should get the Constructors' Championship, and that's good for the firm."

"What did Carlo mean when he said, 'here of all places'?"

"This is the *Italian* Grand Prix. For Valetti it's the big one. The firm is expected to win here. If it doesn't the *tifosi* may riot."

"That's a word I haven't learned yet. What are *tifosi?*"

"Literally it just means the fans, but it's more like a mob. After the race they invade the track to strip souvenirs off the cars, sometimes when they're still moving. One year a Valetti winner had the car dismantled beneath him. They even snatched off his crash helmet, almost with his head still in it. That's what they do if they're pleased. But if Valetti loses—*ai-ai-ai!* Then we get away quick before they catch us."

Serena laughed at Gita's droll expression, but all her sympathy was with Carlo, who would be hurt by his countrymen's displeasure. She returned to her own room, where Carlo arrived later, looking disconsolate. "Gita explained to me about why Monza is important," she told him.

He sighed. "Well, I don't think we're going to win. Ferrando's a sound driver but he can't challenge the Neapolitan when the going gets rough." As he said, "the Neapolitan" Serena felt again all his hatred of Primo, and his galled pride at the prospect of his winning this particular race. "Ferrando's best hope is to do a fast qualifying time tomorrow," he went on. "Will you be there?"

He wasn't looking at her, and she wondered if she imagined that he held himself tense as he waited for her answer. She had no doubt what it was to be. If Carlo was going to have a bad day, she was going to stick around. "I'll be there," she said at once, and hoped she really had seen a slight relaxation in his shoulders.

She was as good as her word, accompanying him to the pit next morning. The place was already full of bustle, with mechanics checking the car down to the smallest detail, and testing the radio in the driver's crash helmet, through which he would keep contact with the pit. Ferrando, a pleasant but nondescript young man, appeared nervous at the responsibility placed on him.

To Serena's surprise the huge tires were enveloped in material. "They're electric blankets," Giulio explained. "They warm the tires, so when he goes out there he can get maximum speed at once, without having to waste time warming up."

"I hadn't expected to find the stands packed with spectators today," Serena observed.

"They're connoisseurs. The race may not be until tomorrow, but they know it can be won or lost today. The man with the fastest qualifying lap gets pole position on the grid, which means he can get away first. That's why we have special tires for today. They're very soft, so they hold the road well and give a good speed. They wear out quickly, so we can't use them in the race, but they're vital on the qualifying lap."

The first driver was already out, to the cheers of the *tifosi*. He was a minor competitor and covered the three-and-half-mile circuit in one minute twenty-nine seconds, which brought snorts of contempt from the Valetti pit.

At last it was Ferrando's turn. Pale with tension, he slid into the car. The electric blankets were pulled away from the wheels and he drove off. When he was half-way around the track, Carlo signaled by a grimace that this wasn't going to be good. "One minute twenty-seven and a half," he said. "Viareggi will beat that."

Ferrando returned, looking disconsolate. "It doesn't matter," Carlo said. "You've got another try." As he spoke the mechanics were hauling off the wheels and fitting a set with new tires, which they enclosed lovingly in blankets ready for the second attempt.

Primo went out and completed the circuit in one minute twenty-three seconds, after which he declared that he wouldn't bother with his second attempt. "Considering he's just set a new lap record, you can see why," Ferrando observed bitterly.

"It's too soon to despair," Carlo told him. "Just take it easy."

But Serena could see the young man's tension as he got back into the cockpit for his second attempt. An accident was inevitable and it happened almost at once. Going into a hairpin bend he lost control, hit the curb and turned over, to the accompaniment of howls of anguish from the *tifosi*.

"Ferrando—Ferrando—" Carlo cried sharply into the radio.

To everyone's vast relief Ferrando's voice came back immediately in a stream of Italian curses. Carlo dashed out of the pit and began to sprint to the scene of the crash. On the television monitor screen Serena could see Ferrando struggle out of his wrecked car and walk a few steps, rubbing his shoulder.

Carlo returned half an hour later. "His collarbone's snapped," he said. "The ambulance is taking him to hospital. He offered to try to carry on, but I couldn't allow it."

Serena's heart went out to him and she laid a hand on his arm. "Gita explained to me how important this race is,'' she said gently, "and now you won't even have an entry. I'm so sorry, Carlo.''

He looked at her as if in surprise. "But of course I have an entry,'' he said. "I'm going to drive the car myself.''

Eleven

"*No.*" Serena had uttered the explosive denial before she was aware. Every fiber of her being was concentrated in protest against this. "It's too long since you raced. You're out of practice," she said frantically.

"I'm still used to great speed, and I know the Monza circuit like the back of my hand," he said. "Giulio, get me Bernardo's car."

Giulio gave hasty orders, and a dozen mechanics jumped into life. Serena took Carlo's arm and drew him aside. "Carlo please . . ."

"You have to understand, Serena. You can't change my mind about this. It's too important. It's something I must do."

"*Why?*"

"Because my honor demands it," he said violently. "Because this is a country where honor still matters. Ask them." He flung a hand out toward the stands packed with the clamorous *tifosi*. "Tell them that the Italian Grand Prix is going ahead without a Valetti car, and watch what happens."

"If they want to cheer an Italian, they've still got Primo," she persisted.

He gave a grim laugh. "Oh yes, the Neapolitan, driving a Dutch car. It's not the same. Besides, I want the Constructors' Championship, and if Valetti doesn't have a single entry in this race, I'll lose too many points. I *need* that championship. I need the prestige and the sales it can bring the firm."

He looked up sharply as a figure appeared in the entrance of the pit. It was Primo. He stood leaning negligently against the jamb, a look of jeering amusement on his face. "Hey, Valetti," he called, "it looks like you're out of it."

Carlo turned on him. "You'd like us to be out, to give you a clear field."

Primo shrugged. "I don't care either way. Your drivers can't cope with me any more than you could."

Carlo's lips tightened, and there was an ugly look in his eyes. Serena put up a hand, fearful that he'd go for Primo again as he'd done in the casino, but he stood motionless as Primo gave them a cheery wave and walked away. "That man needs teaching a lesson," he said in a soft and deadly voice.

"That's it, isn't it?" she said angrily. "All the other reasons are just a front. What you really want is to 'make him eat his words in dust.'" He was silent, looking at her. "Why don't you admit it?" she cried.

"Does it make any difference?"

She was in despair. His very calmness told her it would be impossible to budge him an inch. "Tell me something," she begged. "Why?"

"Why do I want to even the score with Viareggi? Do you need to ask?"

"Is it because of Dawn—or Louisa—or—?"

He shrugged. "Does it matter? Just let me cross the line ahead of that man, and I'll have restored my honor."

"Honor? Or pride?"

"Is there a difference?"

"Yes," she insisted passionately.

"Serena, you're English. You see things through English eyes. But I'm a Roman and this is Italy, and here there is no difference."

Giulio came to say the car was ready. Carlo went off to get changed, and reappeared a few minutes later dressed in white overalls. Serena watched helplessly as he slid down into the belly of the vehicle and fitted the great helmet on. A few minutes later the car glided out toward the track, and everyone in the pit gathered around the monitor screen. "He's taking it fairly slowly while he remembers the track," Giulio observed. A few minutes later Carlo returned, having lapped in one minute and twenty-nine seconds.

As soon as he got out of the car he plunged into discussion with the team who crowded around, offering advice. Serena watched, feeling like an outsider. Carlo didn't approach her, and she wondered if he knew she was there anymore. He couldn't have told her more clearly she would be no help to him.

His second call came. This time everything was different. He had the feel of the track now, and the time for great caution was over. He spun up to top speed and brought the car in at a minute twenty-four seconds to the accompaniment of screams of ecstasy from the *tifosi,* and roars of congratulations from his team. Only

Serena stayed apart, in a black hell of fear. At last she couldn't stand it anymore, and ran from the pit, not caring where she went as long as it was away from the smell of oil and heated tires. When Carlo looked for her she wasn't there.

When she could force herself to come back, she found an atmosphere of celebration. Carlo had achieved second place in the grid. She tried to seem pleased for him, but inside her she was stunned by what was going to happen. She, better than anyone, knew that this was more than just a race. The two men hated each other, and for each it was a matter of deadly pride to win. Who could predict what the outcome of such a contest would be?

She left Carlo supervising detailed tuning of the engine and returned to the hotel alone. She had dinner with Gita and Louisa, neither of whom seemed perturbed. Gita had seen her son race and survive before, and Louisa regarded it all as a game. There was no one who shared her horrible certainty of disaster.

Alone in her room, she couldn't stop brooding. She'd seen how Primo drove. She realized that he cared for the safety of others as little as he cared for his own. And Carlo knew it. Deep within her a voice was saying that if he had loved her he would have listened to her pleas. But he didn't love her. He'd never pretended to. All the love was on her side, and the anguish if he died.

He returned late, flushed and exhilarated. She waited in bed while he showered the grease off and got in. But when he reached out, she flinched as if a dead man had touched her. "I'm sorry," she said in helpless misery. "I can't . . ."

"You're quite right," he said after a moment. "It's going to be a heavy day tomorrow. Let's get some sleep."

As he was getting dressed the next morning, Carlo said, "They've built a new stand here since last year. You'll be very comfortable in our box."

"Can't I come to the pit with you?" she asked.

"Better not. Gita and Louisa will be in the box. I think you should be with them." It was as polite a snub as a man could give.

She wanted to say something but he was holding the door open for her. "Carlo..."

"Let's hurry," he said, smiling blankly.

There was nothing to do but walk out into the corridor and down the stairs to where everyone was waiting, and there would be no more chance of a private word with him. And when she saw him drive away to the racetrack her heart was full of the things she'd wanted to say, and she could only pray that there would be another chance to say them.

The Valetti private box was the largest and most glittering in the stand. When Serena arrived it was already full of racing luminaries, most of whom she'd never met before. The champagne was flowing, and Gita cheerfully took over the duties of hostess. Serena talked and smiled mechanically, but her thoughts were in the pit with Carlo. As the clock ticked toward two, she imagined him making last-minute checks, getting into the car, slipping on his helmet, not thinking of her because she'd failed him.

There was a map of the racetrack on the wall. She surveyed it, trying not to be sickened by the tight curves where drivers would slow down to 140 mph, and the long straights where 210 mph was common.

"It's marvelous, isn't it?" said someone behind her.

Serena turned and saw a man she recognized as a veteran racing driver, although she couldn't remember his name. "Best track in the world," he went on enthusiastically. "It's got the fastest corners, you see. Especially these two—the Lesimo corners, one straight after the other. You start with a chicane, here—" he pointed to where the straightness of the track was broken by what looked like a squiggle "—and as soon as you're out of that you go into a full-scale bend that immediately becomes another bend, turning right back on itself, so if you make a mistake you can spin off. I did that once and the engine broke right off the back of the car. Hairy. Great fun, though." He chuckled and went off to buttonhole someone else.

It was time. The cars were gliding to their places on the grid, Primo's blue-and-yellow car in pole position, Carlo's distinctive white-and-green vehicle to his left and a few feet behind. The official dropped the flag and the thirty cars streamed away to start the first of fifty-one laps. In the box more champagne was poured, and there was loud cheering.

Primo got away in the lead with Carlo directly behind him. For the first four laps they held these positions. Then it happened. Carlo roared into the chicane before the Lesimo corners, challenged Primo through the chicane and slid past him as they emerged from the second corner. The stadium erupted with joy. Serena sent up a prayer that he would lengthen his lead so that there would be no confrontation.

But having got in front he couldn't pull away. Primo's repeated efforts to pass him were frustrated, but he hung on.

"Viareggi is starting to lose his temper," the veteran said, looking over Serena's shoulder. "That's good."

"Why is it good?" Serena demanded.

"Because he'll probably do something stupid," he explained as if stating the obvious.

The fear in her heart grew. Primo wouldn't care what he had to do to win this race.

Three more laps. The positions were unchanged as they came up to the Lesimo corners, but as they went into the chicane Primo was inching forward. He drew level just as they reached the first corner and his car began drifting sideways, closer to Carlo's.

"Bad," said the veteran briefly. "Reckless driving. Should be a steward's inquiry afterward."

Serena barely heard him. She was holding her breath as the two cars went neck and neck into the second corner, and by now there was no doubt in anyone's mind. Primo was making a barefaced attempt to drive Carlo off the track. A hush fell in the box. Serena's nails were ground into her palm as she sent Carlo a frantic, silent plea to give way.

But she knew he wouldn't. He held his position, refusing to be intimidated. Watching the monitor screen, she thought she saw Primo turn his head as if in amazement that his tactics had failed, and in that split second he drifted the fatal inch too far. The wheels of the cars locked together and the next moment they were both in the air, turning over and over.

Serena moved fast to seize Louisa and hide the child's face against her. When she looked back to the track there was only dust to be seen. Marshals were racing toward the scene. People were screaming. Flags were being waved to stop the race. Serena was cold from shock. She closed her eyes but nothing could wipe out the picture of the two cars spinning madly in the air in horrible slow motion.

She sat without moving, holding the sobbing Louisa in her arms. Every instinct wanted to run to Carlo, but to stay near a phone was the quickest way of learning the truth. In her heart, though, she was sure she knew it. No man could survive such a crash. In a moment the phone would ring and her life would be over.

It was Gita who took the call. Everyone watched as her face relaxed and she whispered, *"Grazie di Dio."* She dropped the receiver and said, "Carlo is alive." She raised her voice above the rejoicing to add, "but he's very badly hurt. They're taking him to the hospital."

Stewards shepherded them out of the building, fighting off *paparazzi* determined to get a good picture of Carlo Valetti's new wife who might soon be his widow. In the car on the way to the hospital, Serena stared unseeing out of the window, refusing to let herself think. The only reality was the child in her arms, who needed her now.

The wait in the featureless hospital room seemed endless. Louisa sobbed herself to sleep, leaving Gita and Serena looking at each other. Gita's well-preserved youth seemed to have fallen away.

A doctor came in. Afterward Serena couldn't remember his name, what he looked like, or anything except what he said. "Signor Valetti has broken ribs, cuts and bruises. But he also received a very heavy blow on the head. He's still unconscious and shows no signs of awakening. I'm afraid that's a bad sign."

"Can I see him?" Serena asked quietly.

''Only for a moment.''

When she entered Carlo's room she had to press her hands over her mouth to keep from crying out. He was linked to machines on both sides of the bed, one to help his breathing, one to monitor his heart, and several others whose function she couldn't guess. His face, wherever it wasn't discolored by bruises and abrasions, was deathly pale. She longed to kiss that still face, but she couldn't get past the machines. After watching him for several minutes with her heart in her eyes, she turned away.

Sitting in the waiting room, she lost track of time. The light outside the window faded and became black. The surgeon came to ask her to sign consent forms. She heard the words, ''Internal bleeding . . . pressure on the brain . . . urgent operation.'' She signed and he went away.

She had no hope. This was just a delay of the inevitable. If he'd gone into that race knowing that she loved him she would have had hope. But she'd turned away from him when he'd reached out, and she hadn't found the courage to speak the next morning. So he would die, and she would always feel as though she had killed him. Her heart was like a stone in her breast.

Giulio came in to say that Primo had been killed outright. She heard the news without interest. Nobody mattered but Carlo.

Night became morning. The surgeon returned. The operation had been a technical success. The pressure had been relieved and Carlo was holding his own.

''I want to see him.''

''Just for a moment.''

This time his head was swathed in bandages, and there were more machines than ever. To her frantically seeking eyes it seemed that his color was a little better and his breathing easier, but he lay frighteningly still.

When she returned to the waiting room Louisa had awakened. "Is Papa getting better?" she asked.

Serena tried to find words of reassurance, but she wasn't quick enough, and her face told the tale. Louisa didn't cry this time, but she put her arms about Serena and held her tight. "Mama..." she said. "Oh Mama...Mama..."

Serena enfolded her. "Yes, *piccina,*" she said, using Carlo's endearment. For a moment she'd been surprised, but at once she knew she shouldn't have been. Louisa had given her the key to endurance, and even to peace. If the worst happened she had a child who needed her. She'd thought of her only as Dawn's child, but at this moment she thought of her as Carlo's; not by blood but by the stronger and more binding tie of love. For Louisa's sake she could be strong if she needed to be. It might be the only thing she could do for the man she loved.

Valeria came to collect Louisa, promising to take her home and care for her. The hours dragged by.

"Don't you want to go in, Gita?"

"No, *cara*. That's your privilege. I have no right."

"But you're his mother."

Gita smiled sadly. "Yes. I'm his mother. But I haven't been a mother to him. I failed him."

"I feel as if I did, too."

Gita shook her head. "No, not you. You love him too much ever to fail him. That's why you're the one he needs. He's had so little love from those who should have loved him."

A memory tantalized Serena. She pursued it to oc-
cupy her mind and stop herself going mad. "I noticed
all those trophies of his father, and none of his own, as
though his father didn't care about him."

"I think he did, in his way," Gita said. "But it was a
very cold way. He never showed his son any affection,
never praised him. Carlo struggled to be a great driver,
because achievement was the only way to win Emilio's
heart, but no achievement could ever be enough. He
wanted his father's love so much." She sighed. "Has
Carlo told you about me?"

"He said you went away when he was twelve," Serena said hesitantly.

"*Si.* I went away," Gita said wryly. "I abandoned my
son because I was unhappy, and too selfish to see what
I was doing to him. I wrote to him, but the letters came
back. Then one day he simply arrived on my doorstep.
He was twenty. He'd forgiven me because he had no one
else, and he was lonely.

"I invited him to stay, my husband welcomed him,
but Tomaso had just been born, and we three were a
family. Carlo was an outsider. We've stayed on good
terms, but it was too late for me to make amends.

"I hoped for so much for him when he married Dawn
but—forgive me, I know she was your cousin, but she
was a greedy, heartless woman. She married him for his
money, and never gave him any love or warmth.

"Now there is you. I know how much you love him.
He doesn't know, but I do."

"You've seen a good deal, haven't you?"

Gita nodded. "I see that he is afraid of love, and that
is my fault, and his father's, and Dawn's. And I see one
person who can teach him not to be afraid, and that
person is you."

"But how can I reach him now?" she cried.

"I don't know, *cara*. But I do know that if you can't, nobody can."

The first day became the second, then the third and the fourth. The doctor professed himself delighted with Carlo's progress. The patient had come through the operation well and was growing stronger every day. Gradually the machines were disconnected. He breathed easily without help and his heartbeat was strong. But still he didn't wake.

Gita and Tomaso returned home. The second week passed. The bandages were removed, then the stitches, and his hair began to grow back over the wound, giving him an almost normal appearance except that he'd become so thin. Yet still his coma persisted. The doctor had stopped predicting that he'd come out of it at any moment.

"Is there any sign of brain damage?" Serena asked with the courage of desperation.

They were standing by Carlo's bed, and the doctor drew her out of the room before answering. "The tests have shown no sign of brain damage," he assured her. "Physically there's no reason why he shouldn't awake. But these things are unpredictable. It could be at any moment, or—" He shrugged.

"Or never?" Serena forced herself to ask.

"That's being too gloomy. I'm sure he'll awake when he's ready, but only he can tell when that will be."

"Why did you insist on coming out of the room to tell me this? He can't hear us, can he?"

The doctor hesitated. "He might. We know that hearing is the last thing to go and the first thing to return. I've known deeply unconscious patients surface and tell me things I said when they were out.''

When he'd bustled away, Serena returned slowly to Carlo's room and went to the bed. He lay still, breathing quietly. She could reach out and touch him. She could kiss him as she had many times. And yet he was so far away, and only the strength of her love could bring him back to her.

She leaned close to him. ''Carlo,'' she said softly. ''My darling . . . can you hear me?''

Twelve

He was dreaming, and in his dream he saw a face that had haunted him for years, the face of a young woman with light brown hair and large, serious eyes.

It changed almost at once, becoming cold and hostile, accusing him; then smiling, the eyes glowing up into his with joyous abandon. There seemed to be a dozen of her. Now she had wildflowers in her hair and a simple green muslin dress that swirled as she danced. She was sunshine in his arms as they waltzed together, but suddenly they weren't dancing anymore, and she was naked against him, whispering hot passionate words against his mouth as she incited his desire with her own.

But at the very moment he reached out to claim the beautiful vision, it vanished, leaving him alone and desolate in a lunar landscape.

Suddenly the silence was replaced by deafening noise. He was in a small, tight space, surrounded by hot metal and screaming tires. The world flew past outside. Danger rushed toward him and his enemy's face loomed in his consciousness. At some point he'd understood that Primo Viareggi would do anything to drive him off the track. Winning mattered to him that much, because it was all he had. In the same moment, it had dawned on him like a flash of lightning, that winning didn't matter at all to him. His world was elsewhere, in the arms of a woman whose love he still hoped to win.

He'd been ready to brake, pull back, let Primo have the worthless trophy. But it had been too late. He'd felt the shock of impact as they collided, the car lifting from the road and the universe go spinning about him. He'd seen the inevitability of his death in that moment. Now he would never be able to tell her that he loved her. Of all the things for which he would have liked to ask Serena's forgiveness, concealing his love was the worst crime of all.

Her face was there again, smiling, not at him, but at Louisa, in the perfect communication they'd found so easily and which somehow excluded him. All his life he'd been on the outside, gazing longingly from behind an invisible barrier at the warmth and joy others took for granted. He had longed for her to make the barrier vanish and draw him into the warmth, and now he knew he was dreaming again, for her voice was in his ear, soft and husky as he loved it, "My darling, can you hear me?"

In his dream he cried, "Yes," and tried to find her. But she was nowhere. Only her voice reached him through a mist. "Come back to me. I need you. I love you. What will I do without you?"

He could hear the sound of her weeping, and wanted to tell her that it was all right. If only she loved him he'd go any distance to find her. But no sound came from his mouth, and he knew she couldn't hear him.

There was a blankness that seemed to go on for a long time, but at last she was there again. She sounded determinedly cheerful, talking about ordinary things. "Bernardo was better in time to race in Portugal. He won, and he promises to win again in Spain. They asked me whether we should pull Valetti cars out, but I said no. We're going to win the Constructors' Championship, the way you wanted."

He would have liked to tell her that he didn't care anymore, but he knew now that she couldn't hear him, so he lay quietly, listening. The sound of her voice was sweet.

"Louisa comes every day to say hello to Papa, and when we're alone we talk about you. She's told me so many things, and I feel I've really come to understand you for the first time. I wish I'd understood you before, my darling, but if—*when* you get better, it's going to be different.

"The doctor says you can come home soon. Perhaps being in your own room will help. You'll sense the familiar surroundings and—" Her voice grew husky. "Anyway, I'll have you with me."

She seemed to go away, and he felt lost, but after a while she was there again and her voice seemed to caress him. "You're home now. Louisa's so thrilled because it's her birthday today, and she'd been hoping you'd be here in time. I gave her a silver filigree necklace and told her it was from you.

"I miss you so much, darling. Even though you're here in my arms, I miss you terribly. I think constantly about what we'll do when you're better. I have so many plans, and I have to believe that they'll happen one day. But in the end, all the plans come down to one thing, that I want to tell you how much I love you, how much I've always loved you, and always will. Sometimes, over these past few weeks, I've dared to hope that perhaps you loved me, and didn't want me to know because of all the other people who've disappointed you.

"Do you remember that day in England, and the house you bought me, where we met? I think you felt very close to me that night, and one day maybe you will again. It's the hope I live on. Nothing else matters except that you should love me and not be afraid to tell me so."

He thought he heard her weeping again, a lonely, despairing sound, and it was terrible because he couldn't comfort her. But then the nothingness came over him, an engulfing that wiped out everything in the world, that might have lasted for a moment or for a year, and was still there when he opened his eyes.

His mind was completely empty. He saw a room that looked vaguely familiar, and a woman standing by the window. Her back was to the light and her face in shadow, so he couldn't see the leap of hope in her eyes at the sight of him awakening, or the fading of hope as she took in his blank expression. She came toward him. "Carlo?"

For a brief moment he didn't know her. Her face wasn't like any of the faces that had haunted him. It was sad and careworn, as though the fight to keep her courage up had drained all the strength out of her. But some part of him, still buried in a dream, struggled to understand the bittersweet sensation that flooded him at the sound of her voice.

Then she whispered his name again, and suddenly the mist cleared and he knew who she was. He would have opened his arms to her, spoken to her with wonder, but the door opened and Louisa appeared, shrieking at the sight of him awake, and bouncing onto him with joy. He hugged her, but his glance was for the woman who was watching him.

Disappointment was like bile in his throat as he studied her. There was no message of love in her eyes. They were cool and reserved, and her smile gave nothing away. His wits were still too scattered for him to wonder if *she* was studying *him* for some sign. He didn't know that his first glance at her had been a baffled stare that had frozen her hope. He only knew that more than anything he wanted them to be the two people who'd met in the dream place. Instead they were polite strangers.

"You'd better fill me in," he said guardedly. "I don't remember much."

"You crashed at Monza," she said. "You nearly died. You've been unconscious for nearly a month. They let me bring you home a week ago."

He frowned. "I don't remember much about the race."

"The doctor says it's normal if you have a blank spot in your mind."

"Yes." He gave an awkward laugh. "My mind's been playing me tricks lately. Funny, that. Things seem so real and then—it was just your imagination all the time."

He tried to get out of bed and discovered that his old strength wasn't there. "Damn!" he said, furious at being weak.

"You'll need some physiotherapy to get your muscles working again," Serena told him.

"Then the sooner the physiotherapist gets here, the better."

Almost at once, it seemed, his time was filled with the congratulations of well-wishers, matters from the company that needed his decision, and the attentions of medical staff. He welcomed them because they took his mind off the bitter void of disappointment that had been left where her love should have been.

Within a week he was able to get out of bed for several hours a day. In two weeks he was walking about normally. The grand prix season came to an end, with the Constructors' Championship awarded to Valetti Motors. Bernardo and the recovered Ferrando had driven themselves ragged to win it for him, so he praised them and made a pretense of delight. But it meant nothing to him beside the fact that the abyss between himself and his wife grew wider and emptier every day.

At night he waited for her to reach out to him, but she didn't, and he couldn't bring himself to seek her love. The memory of how she'd flinched from him last time acted as a brake.

He noticed, as if from a great distance, that Louisa had started to call Serena "Mama." It pleased him, but the sight of the love that bound them together increased his sense of isolation. When the weather turned cold and he realized that winter would soon be here, he was amazed. It had been winter in his heart for so long that he had almost forgotten anything else.

But just occasionally he remembered a springtime that seemed a lifetime ago, but which was only a few months; the spring when they had stood beneath the trees and looked into each other's eyes and known that they had found each other forever. Only it hadn't been forever.

Sometimes in the night, he would seem to hear her again. *"Nothing else matters, except that you should love me, and not be afraid to tell me so."* Her voice was clearer to him than any reality. Yet he had to accept that she hadn't really spoken to him in his unconsciousness. It had all been an illusion, born of his own hope and love.

One day Serena said, "I ought to go back to England to see Julia. She wants to buy the business from me."

"And you intend to sell it to her?" he asked, with a flash of hope. Severing a tie with England made her seem more securely his.

"I'm not sure," she said guardedly. "I'll make up my mind while I'm there."

And maybe you'll never come back, he thought. *I won't let you go. I dare not.* Aloud he said, "I'll tell my secretary to arrange your flight."

On the day of her departure he offered to drive her to the airport, but she thanked him politely and declined. He spent a wretched day at work, unable to concentrate, waiting for her call to say she'd arrived safely. But of course, he realized, she wouldn't call him here. She'd wait until the evening. He left early and hurried home.

"Mama called," Louisa said as soon as she met him. "She said to tell you she arrived safely."

He gave a forced smile. "That was kind of her." He went upstairs, trying to come to terms with the fact that Serena had chosen to call when she knew he would be out.

For Louisa's sake he assumed a cheerful face for dinner, and had the feeling she was doing the same for him. She'd dressed herself up nicely, with her best new dress and a necklace he'd never seen before, and she kept the conversation going with a determined tact that made her seem old beyond her years.

She's as scared as I am, he thought. *But Serena wouldn't do that. She loves the child, if not me. She'll come back to her. Of course she will.*

He lay awake for most of the night, obscurely troubled by something he couldn't place. Something significant had happened and he'd missed it. If only...

Toward morning he fell into a fitful sleep, and almost at once the "something" fell into place. He awoke to find himself sitting up in bed, shaking with hope and excitement. In a moment he'd thrown on his dressing gown and rushed to Louisa's room.

"*Piccina,* wake up," he said urgently.

"What is it, Papa?"

She sat up and he took hold of her shoulders. "That necklace you wore last night. Where is it?"

She took it from a drawer by her bed and gave it to him, saying reproachfully, "I wore it specially for you, and you didn't notice."

He laid it out across his palm. It was silver filigree. "Where did you get it?" he asked with terrible urgency.

"Mama gave it to me on my birthday. She said it was from you, but you were still asleep and I think she was just being nice."

I gave her a silver filigree necklace, and told her it was from you.

He heard her voice again in his head, so clearly that he almost looked around for her. The woman in his dreams had said those words. And they were true. He hadn't imagined it. But the rest? Had she really said the other things?

Galvanized, he rushed for the nearest telephone and called the airport. Louisa pattered after him and stood watching. When he asked for flight information, she said wisely, "The next plane to England is eleven o'clock this morning, Papa. That's the same one Mama went on."

"Of course it is," he said quickly. "Thank heavens one of us has kept a clear head. Put something on your feet *piccina*. Hello, put me through to Reservations."

"Are you going to bring Mama back?" she asked hopefully when he'd put down the phone.

"Yes," he said, overwhelmed with happiness and relief. "I'm going to bring her back."

He knew Serena had given up her London apartment, so as soon as he landed he went to her office, where he found Julia sitting behind the main desk. And here things began to fall apart.

"Serena?" Julia echoed, puzzled. "No, I haven't seen her. She'd said she was coming soon, but she hasn't been in touch."

"But you must have seen her," he said frantically.

"Signor Valetti, I didn't even know she was in England."

He stared at her in horror. But then the inevitable, the only possible answer broke on him, and he cried out, *"Fool."*

"I beg your pardon!"

"Not you, *signorina,* myself. Fool, idiot, *cretino, imbecille.* Why did I come here, when the truth has been staring me in the face?"

In the late afternoon he reached Delmer and turned the car in the direction of the house. Dusk was already falling and he could see a light on in the house. He found the front door open and went straight in, but a quick search showed him the house was empty. Then a slight movement from the garden caught his eye, and he went out through the French doors.

She was standing beneath the trees, in the place where they'd discovered each other months ago. It had been spring then, and the trees had hung heavy with buds ready to burst into beauty. Now it was the start of winter, and the trees were as bare as the wasteland that had lived in his heart since he'd awoken. But she was there, and when she looked up he saw in her eyes what he had longed to see—the same love and passionate hope that he knew was in his own.

He walked slowly toward her. "What are you doing here?" she asked, as if she was almost afraid of the answer.

"I came because there's something I have to say to you. I love you." He held out his hands to her. "I love you enough not to be afraid anymore. I want to hear you say you love me, as you did so many times in my dreams. Tell me they weren't only dreams."

The feel of her in his arms confirmed it, as did the sweet pressure of her mouth on his. "No," she whispered. "They weren't only dreams. Or if they were, they were my dreams, too. While you were unconscious I opened my heart to you as I never could before. I didn't know if you heard me—"

"I heard everything, but when I came around you were so distant."'

"Only because *you* were. I was in despair, we seemed so far apart. I came here because it was the only place left where I could feel you close to me."

"I'll always be close to you," he promised, kissing her repeatedly, "from now until the end of our lives, and beyond."

A drop of rain fell from the branches above them and touched her face, as it had done once before, in spring. He brushed it away with tender fingers and softly repeated the words he'd said then.

"Come, beloved. Come home with me . . . forever."

*   *   *   *   *

Silhouette Desire

COMING NEXT MONTH

LINDY AND THE LAW
Karen Leabo

Free-spirited Lindy Shapiro was always getting
into and *out of* trouble until she met Sheriff Thad
Halsey. Then the sparks started to fly and,
suddenly, they were both getting *into* trouble!

RED-HOT SATIN
Carole Buck

Hayley Jerome needed a fiancé fast – her mother
was on the way to meet him! Sexy, outrageous,
undercover worker Nick O'Neill volunteered to
play Mr Wrong so he could get closer to Hayley –
much closer!

NOT A MARRYING MAN
Dixie Browning

When a silent five-year-old girl appeared in his
hotel with a note attached to her coat saying she
was his niece, MacCasky Ford had some questions.
Would finding his half-brother's wife answer them?

Silhouette *Desire*

COMING NEXT MONTH

BABY ABOARD
Raye Morgan

Carson James was suave, charming, footloose and
determined to avoid commitment and marriage. So
when he met Lisa Loring, who was looking for a
husband and a father for the children she wanted,
he knew he should buy a one-way ticket out of
town!

A GALLANT GENTLEMAN
Leslie Davis Guccione

Jake Bishop was devastatingly handsome, obstinate
and very good at handing out unwanted advice.
But he wasn't so good at receiving it, especially not
from Kay McCormick, his daughter's pretty sailing
teacher. What would Kay know about emotional
stormy waters?

HEART'S EASE
Ashley Summers

CC Wyatt was a family man without a family, a
gentleman without a lady. Valerie Hepburn was all
that hc was looking for, but would she let her tragic
past prevent a happier future?

COMING NEXT MONTH FROM

Silhouette

Sensation

romance with a special mix of suspense, glamour and drama

THE LETTER OF THE LAW Kristin James
SOMEONE'S BABY Sandra Kitt
SAFE HAVEN Marilyn Pappano
BORROWED ANGEL Heather Graham Pozzessere

Special Edition

longer, satisfying romances with mature heroines and lots of emotion

LURING A LADY Nora Roberts
OVER EASY Victoria Pade
PRODIGAL FATHER Gina Ferris
PRELUDE TO A WEDDING Patricia McLinn
JOSHUA AND THE COWGIRL Sherryl Woods
EMBERS Mary Kirk